As he saw Kerry approaching, ~~~~~~~~~~ ened up with a grin and nudged Wayne in the ribs. Fats looked the other way. 'Well, well, looky here. You're even slower than usual tonight. Is your bag heavy? Can we help you carry it?' Wayne's voice was like poisoned syrup.

Billy's green eyes glowed viciously as he reached out for the bag.

'No thank you,' said Kerry. 'I can manage.' Her heart thumped and she started to tremble.

PETERS
FRASER
&
DUNLOP

503/4 THE CHAMBERS
CHELSEA HARBOUR
LONDON SW10 0XF

AGENT: RC
ROYALTY SHEET No: 17 SS 10700
PUBLICATION DATE: 1990
CATEGORY: CHILD

By the same author:

Copper's Kid

BULLY

Yvonne Coppard

RED FOX

A Red Fox Book
Published by Random Century Children's Books
20 Vauxhall Bridge Road, London SW1V 2SA

A division of the Random Century Group
London Melbourne Sydney Auckland
Johannesburg and agencies throughout the world

First published by The Bodley Head Children's Books 1990

Red Fox edition 1991

Printed and bound in Great Britain
by Cox & Wyman Ltd, Reading, Berkshire

ISBN 0 09 983860 5

1

It would happen again today, Kerry knew it. They would be waiting at the school gate, although of course they wouldn't touch her there. Usually it was just inside the park that they pounced. They would walk beside her, copying her steps exactly: the slow, dragging foot on her crippled leg, and the quick, heavy thump of her good one.

'Hopalong! Hopalong!' they would sing. Then one of them, usually Billy Taggart, who was the biggest of the fourth-year boys, would take her bag, or try to trip her up. And she couldn't run away, and she couldn't chase them, and she couldn't fight, because of her leg, which would not do what she wanted it to.

'Kerry Cripple', they called her, or 'Kerry the Spas'. The children in her own class didn't call her names but some of them pitied her, which was almost worse. No one knew what she had once been, before the accident and the move to this new school, and she wouldn't tell them.

Sometimes, Kerry dreamed about getting her revenge on Billy Taggart. In her dream, she threw herself at him and pushed him to the ground. Her small, thin body became big and strong. She pulled Billy's arm up tight behind his back and forced his face into the gritty black dirt of the path until he begged for mercy.

In the real world, of course, she couldn't fight him. If she lunged at him, he nipped nimbly out of her reach and made her twist on her stiff leg until she tripped. Always she ended up sprawling in the dirt, humiliated and burning with rage and tears. Billy's grinning face, with its sharp teeth, crowed above her. 'Kerry's gone crazy. Crazy Kerry Cripple!' The taunt would follow her across the park, until she came within sight of her own back gate. No, she couldn't fight, and so she fell back on the only defence she had, which was silence. She ignored them, and saved up the tears and rage for her pillow in the dark safety of her own bedroom at night.

One day she would get Billy Taggart, really get him. But that didn't solve the problem of today.

Already, as she saw the hands of the clock creeping round towards half-past three, Kerry felt her stomach begin to churn. Ten more minutes to go. Her knees felt wobbly and the knuckles gripping the pencil turned white. She concentrated hard on the map of Australia, edging it all around with blue sea.

When the bell rang she jumped, and her bad leg jolted against the corner of the desk. She almost cried out, but the hot pain was a familiar one, and would pass.

'Now I want you to finish the map for homework

and give it in at tomorrow's lesson, complete with key. You may go.'

There was a fury of scraping, a clattering of steel legs upon steel legs as chairs were stacked against the wall and tables were cleared.

'Are you all right, Kerry?' Miss Jones hovered over her with a sympathetic smile. All the teachers were sympathetic. They let Kerry go for lunch five minutes earlier than everyone else so that she could reach the dinner queue. At break times she was allowed to stay in whenever she wanted to; the others were thrown out into the cold school yard with hearty cries from the teachers: 'Go on – hurry up out. The fresh air will do you good.' (Fresh air, it seemed, was only good for children – the teachers went off to the warm staff room for a hot drink and a cigarette.) Kerry knew they were just being kind, and so she didn't feel able to tell them that she would prefer to be treated the same as everybody else.

'I'm all right,' muttered Kerry. 'Thank you.' She could feel Miss Jones' eyes on her as she limped to the door and followed her classmates out to the playground.

'Are you all right, Kerry?' It was June Richards, who had been put in charge of Kerry when she first arrived at the school, to show her around. Kerry had resented being looked after, and was fed up with being asked the same question, over and over, as if she were a baby – 'Are you all right?'

'I would be,' she snapped, 'if people would just leave me alone!'

June shrugged and walked away, laughing easily

at a shared joke with a small group of her friends. June was pretty, and popular, and did not need Kerry's approval. Kerry wished she hadn't been so hasty. June might even have walked home with her – they lived very near to each other – and saved her from Billy Taggart and his mob. But Kerry walked so slowly she was too embarrassed to ask; whoever walked with her would have to go at a snail's pace or stand, waiting, while Kerry caught up. The unfairness of it burned inside her. It was being so slow that made her easy prey for Billy Taggart.

Sure enough, as she reached the park gates she saw him slouched there, pulling on a cigarette which he was sharing with Wayne Shaw and Fats Wilkins, his hangers-on. Fats was Billy's stooge. Faced with a choice between being constantly picked on or following Billy Taggart, he had become an unwilling slave. Kerry had the feeling he did not like Billy much. His pale, flabby face was not unkind, but he was not clever or brave enough to stand up for himself. Wayne, small and sharp-featured, reminded Kerry of a little terrier. He was by nature spiteful, and quite often was the brains behind some of Billy's schemes. Billy had size and strength, and a taste for humiliating those weaker than himself, and Wayne had a devious mind. Together they were almost unstoppable.

As he saw Kerry approaching, Billy straightened up with a grin and nudged Wayne in the ribs. Fats looked the other way. 'Well, well, looky here. You're even slower than usual tonight. Is your bag heavy?

Can we help you carry it?' Wayne's voice was like poisoned syrup.

Billy's green eyes glowed viciously as he reached out for the bag.

'No, thank you,' said Kerry. 'I can manage.' Her heart thumped and she started to tremble. This was partly fear, but a good deal of it was anger that she should allow herself to be frightened by this pathetic, spotty boy who had nothing better to do than pick on a girl half his size.

'No, no,' said Wayne, with menacing concern. 'We insist, don't we, Billy? We can't have little crippled girls carrying heavy bags like that, can we?'

Billy shook his head. He grinned at Kerry and swiped the bag from her shoulder, roughly, so that she stumbled and almost fell.

The boys started a game of catch with the bag, tossing it through the air and deliberately missing it, so that it fell to the ground. Kerry, knowing she could do nothing, just stood and watched, waiting for them to tire of the game. After a few rounds of catch they started to play football with it. Kerry saw that her books could be torn to pieces by this new activity, and shouted out without thinking: 'Leave it alone, Taggart. I'm going to get you for this one day!'

Instantly she bit her lip. Usually she pretended to be slightly bored by the bullies' antics, knowing that it took the edge off their satisfaction. Now she had played her hand; even she could hear the tremble of fear in her voice.

The boys stopped playing. Wayne picked up the

5

bag and shoved it into Fats' arms. 'Here you are, Fats. The little girl wants her bag back. Shall we give it to her? You decide.'

Poor old Fats swallowed. Kerry could see his heart was not really in it, and so could Wayne. If Fats gave her the bag, he would be a traitor to the group. He had to prove his loyalty. 'No,' he mumbled. 'Let's not.'

'What's that?' grinned Wayne. 'What's that you say, Fats? Can't hear you!'

In a sudden surge of anger, Fats slung the bag as far away from him as he could. It landed with a thud in some bushes. Wayne went to pick it up. Then he stopped, looked down at the ground, and smiled back at them. He dropped the bag again, and then picked it up by the handle, wrinkling his nose. 'Oh dear,' he said. 'I'm afraid a doggy has been this way.' He walked towards Kerry, swinging the bag. She could smell it from a few paces away. He stopped, and dropped it in front of her.

Kerry moved to pick it up, but Billy grabbed her arm and pulled her back. 'Not so fast, Spas.' Kerry looked at him, fighting down her fear and swallowing the tears that were beginning to well up. She wouldn't let him have the satisfaction. She looked around the park. Some distance away, a mother pushed her toddler on the swing; over the other side of the field, a man walked his dog. No doubt they thought this was a shared game, if they noticed the group of children at all. If she screamed, they would probably come over to see what was the matter; but by that time, the boys would have run off and would no doubt have a good laugh about it, not to mention

6

what would happen the next time they caught her alone. 'What now?' she said, trying to copy her father's tone of irritation when someone interrupted his work.

Billy thrust the cigarette towards her. 'Have a drag.'

Kerry shook her head. 'I don't smoke.'

'I don't smoke,' mimicked Wayne in a high-pitched voice. The other two laughed.

'Want your bag back?' asked Wayne.

Kerry nodded.

'Then smoke it,' said Wayne. 'Give her a hand, lads.'

He took the cigarette from Billy, and Billy took one of her arms, motioning to Fats to do the same. As Kerry opened her mouth to protest, Wayne stuck the cigarette between her lips and she automatically clamped her teeth on it to stop it being rammed down her throat. Then she spat, as hard as she could, sending the disgusting thing flying into the air.

'You've had it now,' said Wayne gleefully. 'That was Billy's last ciggy, and you've ruined it . . . .'

'Someone's coming,' squealed Fats.

A man and a woman, the man holding a large Alsatian on a lead, turned into the gate nearest them. The boys sauntered off in the opposite direction, trying to look casual. Their steps were a little quicker than usual.

Kerry looked miserably down at her bag, with its great smear of dog dirt. Tears ran down her cheeks.

'Are you all right?' The woman put her hand on Kerry's shoulder.

7

'Yes,' said Kerry. If one more person asked her that question, she would kill them, she thought.

'Were you having trouble with those lads?' asked the woman.

Kerry shook her head. 'I've dropped my bag, that's all,' she said.

The man picked up the bag, wrinkling his nose in disgust, and took it off to find some large leaves. He wiped the worst of it off, and brought it back. 'How far have you got to go?' he asked kindly.

'My house is only over there,' said Kerry, pointing to the other side of the field. Her house backed on to the park. It made the bullying even more humiliating, somehow, that she could see her home and safety all the time it was happening, but it might just as well have been on the other side of the world.

'Are you sure you'll be all right?' asked the woman again.

Kerry nodded her head. 'Thank you very much,' she said. 'I'm fine now, really.'

The couple paused and looked at each other. Then they walked off, the Alsatian trotting obediently by their side.

Kerry dragged the bag along the path. She just hoped the books were all right. Luckily, Mum would not be at home for an hour or so after Kerry today; she had an appointment in town, and had given Kerry the door key. It would give Kerry a chance to wash her face and clean up her uniform. She doubted that the bag could be properly cleaned up and repaired, though. She would just have to tell her parents that she had stumbled and the bag

8

had gone flying into bushes. They would buy her a new one without much fuss. After all, poor old Kerry couldn't help it if she couldn't keep on her feet any more, could she?

Rage and self-pity sent more tears down Kerry's cheeks. Angrily, she brushed them away. 'One day, Wayne Shaw and Billy Taggart,' she muttered. 'One day, I swear, I am going to get you!' She limped off down the path.

2

The next day, Kerry arrived at school with her books in a plastic carrier bag. Billy Taggart, standing in a corner of the school playground, noticed it at once. He nudged his cronies, and they sniggered.

Her mother had pointed out that her gymnastics-club kit bag was a perfect substitute for the ruined one, but Kerry had refused to take it out of the house. 'A cripple with a gym bag? That'll give them something to laugh about at school.' She had instantly regretted the remark when she saw her mother's face. Mum had been driving the car when it crashed. No one quite knew why the car had left the road, but Liz Hollis had never forgiven herself for being the one to step clear of the wreckage with only cuts and bruises, while Kerry had been trapped for three hours until firemen freed her crushed leg.

Kerry hugged her mother fiercely, trying to squeeze out the guilt that stood between them, making it impossible for her to confide anything to do with the accident, or her leg, or the gymnastics she had been forced to give up.

'You're not a cripple, Kerry.' Her mother's eyes were filled with tears.

'Of course I'm not,' said Kerry. 'I'm just feeling sorry for myself, that's all. And I'm cross about the bag.'

Her father, who had been collecting his jacket to go to work, came into the kitchen just as she said this. 'I'll buy you a new bag on the way home from work tonight,' he said. 'Though I feel bound to point out that in my day we were only too glad to have a carrier bag each. Why, there were days when my brother and I had to choose who would go to school, since there was only one plastic bag between us . . . .'

'Oh, Dad,' groaned Kerry. Her father, who had actually lived a very comfortable life as the son of a wealthy stockbroker, had a sense of humour which was beyond her understanding sometimes.

Dad laughed and ruffled her hair. ''bye, kiddo. See you tonight.'

'Don't worry about the bag,' said Mum. 'But perhaps the walk to and from school is a bit much for you right now. Would you like me to take you in the car?'

Kerry shook her head. 'No. Honestly, Mum, I wasn't tired, just not looking where I was going. My leg will never get strong if I don't use it. I enjoy walking to school,' she lied, and her mother's face brightened.

'Well, as long as you're sure. I expect you appreciate the chance to chat to the other girls on the way, just as I did at school.'

Kerry smiled at her and went to get her coat.

Her mother assumed that Kerry had found making friends as easy here in this new place as she had always found it at home – not home now, she corrected herself quickly, the old place. In fact, since Kerry was not willing to give away anything about herself, the other girls had lost interest in making friends. 'Touchy' had been the general verdict on the new girl. Kerry was intelligent enough to understand that she deserved the title.

All day the indignity she had suffered at the hands of Billy and the others burned in her, making her even more distracted and standoffish than usual. A group of girls came up to her at break and asked her if she was all right, and she nearly snapped their heads off. She turned round to say 'sorry' and start again, but by that time they were on the other side of the playground, and she was too proud to hobble across to them and risk being rejected.

As three o'clock approached, the familiar churning started in her stomach. She watched the clock tick round towards the half-hour. They were supposed to be in small groups discussing their views on school uniform. Kerry's contribution had been, 'It's all right, I suppose,' after which they had given up trying to involve her and she had been left on the edge of the group, daydreaming about how she could get back at Billy Taggart, and building up her fear of what would happen after school.

When the bell rang and the children poured out of the class, Kerry saw Miss Jones bearing down on her. Her heart sank. What now?

'Are you all right, Kerry? Is anything wrong?'

Kerry gritted her teeth. She wanted to swear. Why did everyone have to ask that same, stupid question?

'I'm all right,' muttered Kerry. 'Thank you,' she added hastily, but Miss Jones had settled herself on the edge of the desk. Clearly Kerry was in for some kind of heart-to-heart; she could tell by the expression on Miss Jones' face. Miss Jones was Head of Second Year, as well as teaching them geography. When Kerry had first arrived she had talked to her for a long time about how she understood what Kerry must have been through, how unsettling it was to move house and school after going through such a 'terrible time'. She didn't actually mention Kerry's leg, or the accident, or the six months in hospital that meant she had to start the second year all over again when she should be in the third. It was all condensed into the phrase 'terrible time' as though it had been a short spell of unpleasantness that was now over.

'You've been here nearly a month now, Kerry, and your work is excellent – I hear only good reports from the other teachers. But you don't seem happy, dear. You don't seem to have made many friends. The report from the last school said you were a happy, popular child, always willing to join in school activities. Is there a problem you would like to talk to me about, Kerry?'

'No, Miss.' Kerry stared at the floor. Her dark hair swung forward and hid her face. Fat lot of use it would be telling Miss Jones about Wayne Shaw and Billy Taggart – she would tell them off, the Headmaster would have a go at them, and Kerry would cop it when the heat died down. Not only would she be Kerry the Cripple, but Kerry the Snitch, Kerry the Coward, as well.

'I'm here to help, you know, Kerry,' said Miss Jones in a low voice. 'They do say a problem shared is a problem halved.'

'I'm all right, honestly.' Kerry met Miss Jones' eyes, and then looked away. Miss Jones was not easily fooled.

There was silence for a moment, and then Miss Jones tried another tack. 'Have you joined any school clubs yet, Kerry?'

'No, Miss.'

'Do we have nothing that interests you? There's something going on every dinner time, isn't there? What about the choir?'

'Can't sing, Miss.'

'Or the guitar group?'

Kerry shook her head.

There was another pause and then Miss Jones said carefully, 'There's always the gymnastics club, of course.'

Kerry shot her a look of pure disbelief. 'Don't be daft!' she exclaimed. 'Sorry,' she added hurriedly.

'I'm not being daft, Kerry. Fair enough, you can't do the moves yourself any more. But you were a junior champion, all set for the national team and even the Olympics one day, they said. Your mother showed me a newspaper clipping of the last competition you won, before the accident. You were very good.'

'Yes, I was,' said Kerry bitterly, a cold rage

14

building inside her. 'But haven't you noticed? I can't even walk properly now!'

Miss Jones didn't seem to hear her. 'As I say, you couldn't compete yourself but you have a lot of expertise you could offer the school team. You've been coached by experts. Mrs Tyson does her best, but gymnastics isn't her speciality. You could help a lot with coaching. I know she would be delighted to have you in the club – so would the other gymnasts, if you told them the truth about yourself.'

Kerry was silent. There was no way she could explain how she felt about going into a gym and watching others do what she could once do. Everyone claimed to understand, but no one really did. Even talking about it made her throat feel tight. That was why no one at school knew she had been a champion gymnast – except Miss Jones and maybe one or two other teachers who had read the reports from her previous school. So far they had respected her need to keep that part of her past a secret.

'Perhaps it's time you stopped nursing your wounds, Kerry, and got on with life, eh? You can't go on like this for ever, can you?'

Kerry shrugged. She was crawling with embarrassment, and wished the old woman would just leave her alone. But there was to be no mercy. Miss Jones droned on, seemingly unaware or uncaring that Kerry wasn't listening: she was just waiting for her opportunity to get away.

'So you will try and take a more active part in school life, won't you, dear?' she finished finally.

'Yes, Miss.'

15

'Good girl. Now.' She looked at her watch. 'I've kept you rather a long time, and your mother may worry about you being late. I'll give you a lift home, Kerry – I go past your door.'

Kerry weighed up the torture of being trapped in Miss Jones' car while she droned on some more, against the bullies who might still be waiting for her at the park gates. 'Thank you, Miss.'

As they drove past the park Kerry waved and smiled very sweetly to Billy Taggart, who was skulking at the entrance on his own. Then she stuck her tongue out at him. She felt a surge of triumph at the expression on his face, even though she knew it would only make him worse the next time.

Kerry's mother was in the kitchen. There was a smell of baking. Three warm loaves stood on the baking rack and a box of small cakes stood ready for the freezer. As Kerry walked in, the bell on the cooker rang and her mother drew out a large chocolate cake.

'Hello, sweetheart. Good day?'

Kerry nodded, knowing that Mum wouldn't be able to cope with the truth. 'Anything to eat, Mum?'

It was Freezer Day. They had one every month or so, when her mother would spend the entire day in the kitchen, filling the house with delicious smells of things no one was allowed to eat. Kerry and her father could drool at the mouth for all Mum cared. Everything would be wrapped up and stored in the freezer for another time – except the cookies. Mum always made them on Freezer Day, whether it was baking or dinners that she was freezing. They were piled on another rack, which her mother now indicated with a movement of her head, while she removed the steaming chocolate cake from its tin. Sometimes, the bottom stayed behind in the tin, and Mum would say, 'Oh blast! We can't freeze that one.' Kerry hovered hopefully for a moment, but the cake came out perfectly. Her mother grinned triumphantly. 'Bad luck, Kerry.'

Kerry shrugged, returning the grin, and helped herself to some milk from the fridge. She took the milk and cookies through to the living room. Mrs Hollis followed her.

'So, what have you been up to today?'

'Nothing much. We didn't have proper maths today – Mr Tucker was away. There's a second-year trip to Alton Towers next Thursday, but I asked if I could stay behind and Miss Jones said I could help in the library for the day.'

'Don't you want to go to Alton Towers?' asked Mum quietly. 'I think you could manage it, Kerry. Your leg is getting better, even if you can't see it yourself. You're walking much better than you did.'

'I just don't fancy it, Mum. It takes hours on the coach and, anyway, I've been before. It's not because of my leg, honest.' Kerry looked at her mother's anxious face and smiled brightly. She wished she hadn't mentioned it, but one of the other mothers might have told her anyway, and then she would worry about why Kerry hadn't.

It *was* her leg, of course. Everything came back to that. Her mother just couldn't shake off the guilt of the crash, even though everyone had told her it was not her fault. If Kerry'd had brothers and sisters it would have been easier, but Mum had given

17

up her job after the accident, and her whole life now revolved around Kerry and her father. Kerry felt smothered in some ways, but in others there were things she longed to talk about and couldn't. Neither of her parents wanted to talk about the accident, and Kerry's mother had never looked the same since that awful day when she had offered to drive Kerry to the seaside.

They had only just managed to save the leg; sometimes Kerry wished they hadn't bothered. An artificial leg might even be easier to walk on, and at least it would be less painful, not to mention all the operations she could have missed. She could never say any of this, though. For the sake of her mother Kerry had to be brave, to try and make it seem straightforward.

It was because of Kerry's leg that her parents had decided to move out of the city and start afresh somewhere else. She had to repeat the second year, and that would have been hard at her old school, with all her friends moving up. Then there was the gym, just down the road. Walking past it every day and seeing all her team-mates competing would be too hard, reasoned her parents. So they had moved out to the country, to a new house and a new school.

They hadn't actually asked Kerry if she wanted to move; they had just assumed it would be better. It was Mum who couldn't bear the old place, not Kerry. Kerry could have coped. But she had said none of this, and had tried to look pleased about moving. All her trophies and newspaper clippings and certificates were packed away in a suitcase under her bed. She had refused to unpack them, and her parents had not asked her about it. The kids at school knew she had been in a car crash, and Kerry refused to say any more about herself. So there were no special friends.

'Can I watch television?' she asked. Her mother nodded, and Kerry reached out to switch the set on.

The doorbell rang. 'I'll get it,' said her mother.

Kerry heard her talking for a moment, and then she came back into the room. Her face was beaming. 'It's a friend from school, Kerry.'

Kerry opened her mouth to say she didn't have any friends, and then shut it again. June Richards had followed her mother into the room. They sat next to each other in history and maths, occasionally went to dinner together, but they were not exactly friends. So why was she here?

Liz Hollis smiled indulgently, exulting in the first sign that Kerry was returning to her normal social life. 'Would you like some chocolate cake, June? I've just made one; it's still warm.'

June nodded and Kerry watched, open-mouthed, while her mother carried in the cake and sliced it for them. 'I thought that was for the freezer,' she said.

'It was, but having a friend round for the first time is a bit of a special occasion, isn't it?' Mum beamed at June, who blushed and looked embarrassed.

They stood looking at each other in an uncomfortable silence.

'Well, I'll leave you two alone. Help yourselves to the cake – and juice, if you want it.' She went back into the kitchen, humming. They heard the faint sounds of pans and bowls clattering as she washed up.

'I saw Old Jonesy taking you home in the car,' said June, 'and I wondered if you were all right.'

'Yes. She just kept me back a bit late.'

'Pep talk? Loyalty to the school, joining in, that sort of thing?'

Kerry nodded, and June smiled. 'She does that to everybody, at least once. I wondered when it would be your turn.' June laughed and threw herself with an easy movement on to the sofa. She had naturally blonde spiky hair. It did not seem to fit in with the deep brown eyes, which sparkled with amusement now as she looked at Kerry.

'*My* crime was getting D for chemistry and maths in the first-year exams, and getting A for history and English. It seems it would have been all right to get C for everything, but to get a mixture of As and Ds says you're not trying. Teachers are crazy, aren't they?' June bit into her chocolate cake. 'So what have you done, Kerry? You're such a hard worker, I can't believe it's real trouble.'

'I haven't joined any school clubs,' said Kerry cautiously. 'She thinks I should.'

''course she does,' snorted June. 'Old Jonesy wants her form to be permanent volunteers, involved in everything. The only club worth joining, by the way, is nature watch – they get time off school now and then to go on one of their rambles collecting weird stones and leaves and other such rubbish. Don't suppose that appeals, though, with your leg being so gammy. Will it get better?'

Kerry was taken by surprise at her directness. Everybody else skated round, asked vague questions, tried to pretend she was not really crippled. Everyone except Billy Taggart, that is. June had never said anything, either. Now here she was asking about Kerry's leg as though it was a perfectly easy and natural topic of conversation.

'I'll probably always limp a bit,' said Kerry. 'A lot of the bone was smashed, and they had to do grafts and stuff. But it will be a lot better than it is now, in the end.'

'Oh, well, in that case my advice is join nature watch. It's a laugh.' She looked at her watch and crammed down the rest of her cake. 'Look, I've got to go – the old dear wants me to take my little sister to Brownies, and then I have to be around to pick her up. I look after her most evenings until my dad gets in, while Mum serves up dinner to the nobs at the golf club. Why don't you come round tomorrow? You can keep me company. Come about six – the old dear will be gone by then. You can have tea with me, if you like.'

'All right,' said Kerry. 'Thanks. And thanks for coming round.'

June smiled. 'It was my dad's idea, really. I told him how weird and standoffish you were at school, and he said he didn't blame you if everyone was as nosy as me. Doing the second year again isn't exactly a bundle of laughs, without having to change schools and get stared at by a lot of strangers. Dad said I ought to try you out on your home ground. Seeing you in old Jonesy's car just gave me the excuse I needed to come over. We're a bit old for me to call and ask if you're coming out to play.'

Kerry laughed, the first time she had laughed properly in ages. 'I'm glad you came. I will come over tomorrow – I'll bring some of my records, if you like.'

She waved June off, and went back into the kitchen carrying the empty plates and the remains of the cake. Her mother was hovering, a question in her eyes. 'She seems a nice girl,' she said. 'Is she in your class?'

'Yes,' said Kerry. 'I'm going over to her house for tea tomorrow. Is that all right?'

Kerry's mother beamed broadly. 'Yes, of course. I'm just glad to see you settling in so well. It's all working out nicely, isn't it?'

'Yes,' said Kerry, and forced another smile of reassurance.

'It's ham salad for tea tonight – do you want it now, or would you rather wait until Dad comes in?'

'I'm too full of chocolate cake to think about tea,' said Kerry. 'Anyway, I've loads of homework to do. I'd better get it out of the way now.'

'Perhaps you shouldn't be doing too much homework,' said her mother anxiously. 'Would you like me to write a note?'

'Oh, Mum, for heaven's sake,' groaned Kerry.

Her mother smiled sheepishly. 'Sorry. Just keep forgetting you're able to look after yourself these days.'

'I know. It's all right.' Kerry picked up her carrier bag and climbed the stairs to her room. She locked the door, and sat on the bed. 'You could help a lot with coaching,' Miss Jones had said.

Kerry remembered the way she had felt on the bars: weightless, beautiful, completely in control of her body as it flew and dipped and twisted in the air. She would never do that again, never feel that sense of power again. She had not considered passing on her skills to someone else; coaching was something you did when you were too old to compete. Yet Miss Jones seriously believed she could help the school gym team. Perhaps she was right. The real question was, how could Kerry bear to stand on the sidelines?

Kerry dropped to the floor and pulled out the old brown suitcase. It was all there: cups, medals, certificates, and a scrapbook of clippings from the local paper. There was also a complete national newspaper which had a picture in it of Kerry winning an Individual Junior Championship. She was only nine years old then, and already the caption claimed she was a promising Olympic competitor. Kerry had not cut up the paper, as she usually did; she was proud of having her name in a national paper, even if it was only a small paragraph near the back.

Idly she leafed through the pages, reading some of the other stories. A pop star had died that day, and three people had been killed in a fire. The Queen had been in Australia, and . . . what Kerry read next, halfway down page seven, made her heart stop for a moment. She read the article twice, three times. It couldn't be. But it all fitted. It had to be . . . .

Kerry smiled. The question of whether or not she should offer her services to the gym club faded into insignificance. What she read was far more important. It was better than getting chocolate cake which should have gone in the freezer, better even than finally having the chance of a real friend. What she read in that old newspaper made her heart sing, because it could solve her biggest problem of all.

Carefully she drew a line around the article with a coloured pencil. She folded up the newspaper and placed it in her bag with her schoolbooks. 'Just you wait, Billy Taggart,' she murmured, hugging herself with glee. 'Just you wait.'

3

The following day dawned sunny and clear, as if it had noticed how much happier Kerry felt and was smiling down on her. Kerry ate her breakfast and gathered her books with more enthusiasm than she had felt for a long time – since the accident, in fact. The knock-on effect of her cheerful smile – really cheerful, not just a pale shadow of an attempt – was that her father kissed her mother and went off to work whistling, and her mother sang as she cleared the table.

The door bell rang. 'I'll get it,' called Kerry. She was surprised to see June.

'Hello. Thought we could walk to school together.' June noticed Kerry's frown, and said frostily, 'Not if you don't want to, of course.'

'I do,' said Kerry hastily. 'But I don't think it's a good idea. I'm . . . well, I can only walk slowly – I won't be able to keep up.'

June laughed. 'Is that all?' she said. 'Why do you think I'm so early? I'm not thick, you know – I allowed plenty of time for the old gammy leg. Come on – I'm quite happy to dawdle. Who's eager to get to that place?'

25

Kerry's mother was standing behind Kerry in the doorway, and she gave her a little push. 'Off you go, then. Here's your bag.'

Kerry took the new bag her dad had bought her. It was a lovely soft leather duffel-type bag, dark red with a matching purse zipped inside. Mum would have bought an ordinary canvas school bag, but Dad had no idea. He had simply gone for one that looked nice, and not bothered about the price. She felt faintly embarrassed about it. Probably they would think she was putting on airs at school. All the same, she loved the bag, and she clutched it tightly as she thought of Billy Taggart. No way was he going to get this one from her.

'Wow! Posh bag,' commented June. 'Wasted on our place – what happened to your other one?'

Kerry could not bring herself to confide in June, not yet, and so she grimaced and said, 'I dropped it in some dog's you-know-what. It was in the seams and everything – couldn't clean it up properly.'

'Yuk!' said June. 'Mind you, I'd happily drop my bag in the sh – you-know-what if I could get one like yours. No chance from my mum, though.'

'Nor from mine. My dad bought this on his way home from work. He's got a lot of taste, my dad, but no idea about how much things like that should cost. He never looks at price tags – it drives Mum mad.'

'He sounds like one in a million to me,' laughed June. 'I'll have to borrow him next time I need some clothes.'

The discussion about parents lasted most of the way to school. Kerry hardly even noticed Fats Wilkins as he walked past them. In any case, not being with the other two this morning, he went past very quickly, avoiding looking at Kerry. Once again she felt a surge of pity for him. In a way, Fats was bullied just as much as she was. He had simply swapped physical hurt and humiliation for the shame of being an unprotesting slave.

As they neared the school gates, Kerry kept a look out for Billy Taggart – but not with any sense of fear, not today. No, today she could hardly wait to see that spotty face and unintelligent leer. She was going to shift the stupid smile off his face, all right.

To Kerry's disappointment, Billy was not at the school gates. It was break time before she spotted him. He was leaning against the wall in a corner of the playground. Kerry moved purposefully towards him. As he saw her coming he straightened up, and nudged Wayne. There was something about the way Kerry held herself that made them both a bit uneasy. Wayne stared malevolently, as usual, and Billy leered; but they said nothing. Kerry walked right up to them and stood directly in front of Billy.

'I want a word with you, Billy Taggart,' she said.

Billy sniggered. 'Go on, then. Just one word, though – I've better things to do with my time than chat up cripples.'

'What word do you want?' sneered Wayne. '"Hello" would do – bit unimaginative perhaps. You'd get better value out of a long word – "super-califragilisticexpialidocious", perhaps. Or "antidis-establishmentarianism" – that's a good one.' He smiled at Billy, who was howling with laughter.

Kerry did not react at all. 'Get rid of the sidekick, Billy Taggart,' she said.

Billy stopped laughing and eyed her carefully. 'Why should I?'

'What I want to talk to you about is private,' said Kerry.

'Ooh, Billy. Sounds like she fancies you.' Wayne did not make any move.

'I know you used to live in Burfield,' said Kerry, looking at Billy. 'I thought we might chat about that. I met someone who knew your family really well – they asked me to pass on a message.'

Billy instantly went white. For a moment, he froze. Then the mask came back into place. He leaned against the wall again. 'I'll see you in a minute, Wayne, over by the bogs. Yeh?'

Wayne looked as though he was going to protest. Then he shrugged and sloped off. Kerry moved right into the corner of the playground, where two walls met and gave some privacy. A couple of first-years were there, whispering to each other; Billy motioned them away with a sharp jerk of his head. Kerry could see that he was rattled. Of course he didn't know what, exactly, she knew. So he was trying to stay casual and act as though she was being a tiresome little kid. But he was tense, and his eyes narrowed suspiciously when he turned to face her.

'What you on about, then? What message?'

'In a minute,' said Kerry coolly. 'First, let's chat. I didn't know your old man was in prison, Billy. Seems to me I heard you telling everyone he worked on an oil rig way up in Scotland and couldn't get home much. Seems to me that's where you tell people you're going when you're off school sometimes – to see your dad on his oil rig. I've heard some weird names for prison, but that one beats them all.' Kerry felt so full of joy and power she could burst. Billy hadn't moved. He just stood there, looking at the ground, no longer white but a deep, shameful red, almost the colour of the bag her dad had bought.

At last. At last she was getting her own back. Kerry felt like an eagle soaring above its prey. She would paralyse it in her shadow, and then she would swoop.

'So what?' muttered Billy. 'Ain't none of your business.'

'No, you're right,' said Kerry sweetly. 'With me, it's simply idle interest. But some of the others won't like to be lied to. You know, at first I thought, "Why keep it a secret?" You'd think someone like Billy Taggart would be quite proud to have a father in the clink; big, tough-guy Taggart. But then when I heard of the crime he'd committed, I understood. There's nothing very tough about beating up old people and taking their life savings, is there? I heard that even the other prisoners don't want anything to do with your dad. Left one old lady so bad she was in a coma for months, I heard.'

Billy looked at her for the first time. His eyes blazed with anger. 'You heard,' he said, 'but you can't prove.'

It was a sweet moment. Kerry could almost hear the trap clanging shut. She pulled the newspaper, carefully folded, out of her pocket. '*Daily Telegraph*, page seven', she said. 'Shall I read it to you?'

Billy reached out to snatch it, but Kerry was ready for him and put it behind her back. 'You're not very bright, I know,' she said. 'So let me help you a bit by giving you some information. Anyone can get hold of old newspapers. You just need to know the date of the newspaper you want.' She tapped her forehead. 'The date of this one is burned into my brain, Billy. My dad could get me copies of all the nationals as far back as I want them. He's got a whole research department he can use if he wants to. You can take this one from me, if you want to. But I'll just get others.'

Billy folded his arms. He was furious, and he was also very worried, but he was trying hard not to show it. 'What do you want?'

'Want, Billy?' asked Kerry innocently.

'Yeh, want. It's some kind of blackmail, right? I leave you alone from now on or you tell everyone about my dad. Is that it?'

'Not quite.'

'Well, stop wasting my time and spit it out.'

Kerry instantly spat. It landed on his face. He moved towards her with his fist raised and then stopped as she waited, triumphantly, for the blow. He brought his arm down.

'As you have pointed out so many times, I am a poor little crippled girl in need of protection,' said Kerry. 'I am going to take you up on your kind offer. Not only are you going to stop pestering me, Billy, you're going to make sure no one else does.

If anyone so much as name-calls or lays a finger on me, I want them dealt with. OK?'

'You're bleeding joking!' gasped Billy. 'I'm not going to be your minder.'

Kerry shrugged and turned round. 'Don't say I didn't give you a chance,' she said. She had walked two paces when Billy's voice, savage and burning with humiliation, halted her. 'All right.'

She turned again. 'Pardon? I don't think I quite heard you.'

Billy gave her a look of pure hate. 'I said all right. Don't push your luck.'

Kerry sighed. It was perhaps a bit much to expect someone like Billy Taggart to go down on his knees and beg, but she had been hoping for a little more than this. Then she saw Wayne making his way towards them. He looked very suspicious. Kerry turned to Billy, and indicated Wayne with her head. 'I do mean anyone,' she said. 'That includes your wolf-cub friend. You'd better make sure he's nice to me, too.'

'How am I supposed to do that?' growled Billy.

Kerry shrugged and said nothing. She went to stand beside Billy as Wayne came up to them.

'You finished?' he snarled.

Billy looked at Kerry. She nodded. 'Yeh,' he said.

'For the moment,' added Kerry.

Wayne, used to seeing her stoop-shouldered and fearful, looked at her with his mouth hanging open. Then he turned to Billy. 'Have you gone soft, or what? I saw that cripple gob on you. What you going to do about it?' He smiled softly. 'Or are we gonna wait for after school?'

31

Billy didn't answer. Wayne pushed him slightly, and he shrugged his friend's hand off savagely. 'We're not going to do anything,' he said. 'Leave her alone.'

Kerry was enjoying the scene hugely. The bell rang for the end of break and she sighed. 'Sorry, Billy, we'll have to meet another time. We'd better go in now.'

'Piss off, Spas!' snarled Wayne.

Kerry pouted. 'I don't like being called names,' she said. 'And I was brought up to know that swearing in front of a young lady is very bad manners – isn't it, Billy?'

'Shut it, Wayne,' said Billy.

'What? You're just going to stand there and let her – what the hell is the matter with you? Here, you don't fancy her, do you? Not her, not with that twisted leg . . . .'

'I said shut it.' Billy pushed past Wayne so hard that Wayne stumbled and almost fell to the ground.

'Oops-a-daisy,' said Kerry. 'Shall I help you up, little man?' She extended her hand.

Wayne looked from her to Billy and back again. His eyes were popping and his jaw hung open. He looked like a very confused chimpanzee dressed up for a tea party with no party in sight. 'Just watch it, Spas!' he spat, and marched away. Kerry felt the glow of triumph warm her all the way through.

'Think you're clever, don't you?' said Billy. 'But you're not clever enough for him, I'm warning you.'

'But I have you to look after me now, don't I, Billy?' said Kerry.

'Wayne won't be pushed around,' said Billy. 'Not

even by me.' He moved towards her, almost pinning her against the wall. She felt the fear begin to creep into her veins. 'You got a deal,' he said. 'You don't tell about my dad, I'll leave you alone. But Wayne? He's another thing. I can't tell him what to do.'

'You had better do your best, Billy,' said Kerry quietly, 'or what I know about you and your family will be all over school is less time than it takes for you to thump a first-year.'

She could see that Billy was struggling not to hit her. She slid sideways against the wall so that she could get past him, and walked away, leaving Billy staring at the wall. June rushed over to her as she reached the school door. 'I've been looking for you', she said. 'I just saw you with that Taggart and his mobile brain . . . .'

Kerry laughed. 'That describes them exactly,' she said. 'Brainless Billy and Wayne the Mobile Brain. I must remember that.'

'But are you all right?' said June anxiously.

For once, Kerry did not mind the question at all. She linked her arm through June's. 'I couldn't be righter,' she smiled. 'Lead on to maths.'

4

Miss Jones was very heartened to see the improvement in Kerry Hollis over the next few days, and silently congratulated herself on having timed her little conversation with the child just right. In fact, Kerry was the subject of a lengthy conversation one dinnertime, in the staff room. It was generally agreed that she was much more lively in class, had a little group of friends to join up with at break and was often to be seen deep in conversation over lunch, instead of sitting huddled in a corner.

'I don't know what's happened,' said Mrs Tonkiss, who taught history, 'but she seems altogether a different girl from the frightened little shadow who joined us at the beginning of term.'

'She's become very chummy with June Richards,' said Mr Tucker. 'They sit together in maths all the time. I expect that has helped.'

'She's much brighter in PE too.' Mrs Tyson waved her sandwich thoughtfully. 'She used to sit on the sidelines with such a martyred air. Now she offers to keep score, cheers on the teams, and even joins in a little bit from time to time.' She sighed wistfully. 'I was hoping she would show up at the gym club, but I guess that's a lost cause.'

Miss Jones was far too modest to claim credit for this change in Kerry in front of her colleagues, but she glowed with satisfaction. She was confident that another little talk – carefully timed, once Kerry had really settled down with her new-found friends – would result in the gym club having a new member. She smiled a secret, knowing smile into her coffee.

'Well, she's joined one club,' said Ron Watts. 'I signed her up for the nature watch just this morning.'

Sandwiches stopped in midpath. All eyes in that corner of the staff room turned to the biology teacher. He stretched his long legs in front of him and sprawled back easily in his armchair.

'Nature watch?' Miss Jones was mystified. 'But that involves long walks, doesn't it? Tramping through bogs and up hills, striding out across the hills – hardly Kerry's style, surely?'

'She's embarrassed enough about walking down the corridor,' said Mrs Tyson suspiciously. 'So why should she want to sign up for long rambles? She must have a crush on you, Ron.'

Ron pretended to be hurt by the laughter which followed this statement, and then leaned forward to divulge his little piece of gossip. 'Not on me,' he said. 'But she does appear to have acquired an admirer.' He paused for suspense.

'Come on then – who?' laughed Mrs Tyson.

'Well, when she came to put her name down for the club, I explained to her about the walks. She said she knew about that. "I thought I could give it a try," she said, "and if it's too much, just turn back. I have a friend who's going to join with me, so it won't be a problem." Fair enough, I thought, so I put her name down – and Billy Taggart's.'

'Billy Taggart? *Billy Taggart?*' There was a small chorus of disbelief.

'But he's a lout,' wailed Miss Jones, seeing all her good work with Kerry Hollis in danger of being unravelled in one fell swoop. 'He's never supported an out-of-school activity in his life. He's as thick as three short planks nailed together and he's been caught bullying the first-years I don't know how many times. He's hardly made of the stuff of protectors to lame children.'

Ron Watts shrugged. 'None the less, he and Kerry Hollis appear to have something going. I checked with him about it, and he said yes, he wanted to join. I pumped him for a bit more information but he got quite surly. "I said I'd join," he muttered in that clenched way he has when you're demanding his homework for the third time, "and that's that." I didn't probe any further, in case he changed his mind. So, the upshot is that Billy Taggart is going to join our little band and carry Kerry's bag, help her over stiles, haul her up rock faces and presumably hold her hand whenever it's needed. And sometimes when it's not,' he added, amid fresh laughter.

'I can't believe it.' Cynthia Jones shook her head.

A similar sentiment was being expressed in a different way at that very moment in the playground beneath the staff room window.

'I don't believe this,' said Wayne. 'What's got

into you, Bill? The bloody nature watch? I mean, *nature watch*? You've got to be joking. What's it all really about?'

Billy shrugged and met Wayne's stare defiantly. 'I'm fed up of skiving off down the chip shop every dinner time, that's all. It's boring. I thought it might be a laugh to join a club, for once. And with this one, you get time off lessons.'

'You have to be desperate to miss a couple of lessons to go and do that,' said Wayne. 'There's something fishy going on here, Bill. I'm not brainless. Something between you and Kerry Hollis. What's up, eh?'

'Nothin'.' Billy decided the best means of defence was probably attack. 'What's it to do with you, anyway? Since when have I had to ask you whether I should do somethin'?'

Wayne's eyes darkened. 'Never,' he said. 'But you're forgetting who your real friends are.'

'No I'm not. I still go down the town with you, don't I? I still skive off when the fish are biting down at the river. I just wanna do something on my own for a change, that's all.'

'But it's not on your own, is it? That cripple's joined, hasn't she? That's why you're so keen on nature all of a sudden, Billy Taggart. You've gone soft on that stupid kid.'

'I haven't,' said Billy. 'I hate her, if you must know.'

His voice and expression were too savage for Wayne to disbelieve him. If he didn't fancy her, then there must be some other reason he didn't want to get at her after school any more and was

seen hovering around her sometimes. She must have
something on him, that must be it. She must have
discovered something Billy didn't want anyone to
know. Wayne was Billy's best friend, and he didn't
know anything like that. But it suddenly occurred
to him that he didn't really know much about Billy
at all. He knew he had an older brother who was
in the Army and didn't live at home, and a dad
who worked up on the oil rigs in Scotland. Billy
didn't encourage people to come and call for him,
preferring to meet somewhere else. Wayne had been
to his house once or twice, quite a long time ago,
and met his mother. She was a mousy woman, not
the type to have skeletons lurking in the cupboard.
So what could it be? Wayne was mystified. 'Is she
blackmailing you, or what?' he asked suddenly.

Something snapped in Billy. He grabbed Wayne
in a fistful of shirt, tie and jumper and lifted him
off his feet. 'Mind your own bloody business!' he
snarled. 'You're worse than having parents for
asking questions, you are!'

He put Wayne down and there was an embarrassed silence. Billy was sorry for turning on his
friend, but did not want to admit it. Wayne, sensing
he had gone too far, also felt it was wise to go
carefully. He needed Billy, to make up for the size
and strength which he lacked himself. They had
formed a perfect partnership up until now. He could
see it beginning to slip away unless he was very
careful.

'Yeah,' said Wayne finally. 'The chip shop is
getting a bit boring. Listen, do you want to go down

the river tonight? Fats said his dad saw trout there this morning.'

'Yeah, OK,' said Billy, putting an eagerness into his voice which he did not feel, so that Wayne would understand he was willing to stay friends.

Kerry was watching the two boys from a distance. She could sense that they were having an argument, and smiled with satisfaction. But she decided to go easy on Billy Taggart for a while. A split between Billy and Wayne might not be to her advantage. Billy might decide to tell Wayne his secret rather than lose him as a friend. Wayne was evil and devious; he would be capable of finding a way out somehow, and Kerry's power would be broken. Maybe she had taken a bit too much of a risk with the nature watch idea. But she could not resist the opportunity to use her power to make Billy do something really out of character.

'Who are you watching?' said June. 'Not Billy Taggart again? What is it between you two?'

Kerry shrugged. 'Nothing much,' she said. 'He's so stupid, I like to see how far I can make him go, that's all.'

'You enjoy twisting him round your little finger, don't you?' There was no mistaking the distaste in June's voice. 'I wish I knew what makes him such an easy target for you.'

'Target?' Kerry turned in surprise. 'You make me sound like a bully.'

June was about to say, 'Well, that's what you are,' but she stopped. Anyone who saw small, fragile-looking Kerry, with her innocent blue eyes and her twisted leg, would laugh at the very idea that Billy Taggart could be afraid of her. But he was.

June liked Kerry: she was a good friend, and they had a laugh together. She had never seen Kerry be cruel to anyone; quite the opposite, in fact. Kerry was the sort of person who would allow her homework to be copied, share her lunch, cover up for a classmate missing from a lesson and frown on people who laughed at the first-years. But there was something a bit hard about her these days, especially when she was near Billy Taggart, which made June feel uneasy.

Kerry, seeing June's troubled look, laughed and linked her arm through her friend's. 'Never mind Brainless Billy and his mobile brain,' she said. 'Let's go to the library and look at the noticeboard. My dad said if there's anything good on at the cinema this weekend he would take us into town *and* stand us a burger and chips.'

June's frown was replaced by a wistful smile. 'I wish your dad could give my dad a few lessons,' she said. 'Sounds great.'

They went off to consult the noticeboard, each determined, for different reasons, to put Billy Taggart out of her mind. But June found her thoughts returning time and time again to a picture in her mind of two faces: Billy Taggart's, like a captive tiger dreaming of breaking out and eating the keeper, and Kerry's smile of malicious triumph. That smile reminded June of a book she had read, *The Lion, the Witch and the Wardrobe*. She imagined the evil Snow Queen had a smile just like that.

Kerry ignored Billy for the next few days. It was

almost as good to watch him watching her, and wondering what she was going to do next, as bossing him about. It was just a different kind of power. She also loved the way the other kids looked at her as she passed them in the corridor. There was no pity in their eyes now, just a faint bewilderment, or envy. It was becoming known that Kerry Hollis was not to be messed about, unless you wanted to find Billy Taggart waiting for you after school. A third-year who teased her, quite light-heartedly, about having to repeat the second year found her 'friend' waiting to have a quiet word in the cloakrooms at morning break, and generally Billy took his task quite seriously. No one knew why he was so concerned for her welfare. June and Wayne, who were the closest to the pair and knew that they heartily disliked each other, had both worked out that there was some kind of blackmail going on. But any attempts to pump Billy or Kerry for anything further met with no success – and of course there was no chance that June and Wayne would join forces to pool the information they did have.

The most popular opinion was that Kerry had become Billy's girlfriend. No one could work out what the attraction was, but Miss Jones put it down to Kerry needing protection and Billy needing to be needed. She believed the great brute was maturing at last. Billy had been in her form two years ago, and she had done her best to instil in him a more caring attitude to other people. She had become very disheartened, especially after he was suspended for running a protection racket among the first-years, but now, it seemed, her hard work with the lad was at last paying off. It just went to show that you should never give up trying.

So, for a few days, Kerry was content to leave Billy squirming like a fish on the end of the line. She had the power to toss him back or reel him in. It felt good.

One afternoon she came into the biology lab for her last lesson, to find her usual place next to June occupied by Susie Mason. She approached the bench with a half-smile, expecting Susie to move to another desk, but Susie stayed right where she was, with the triumphant expression of a queen bee. Kerry looked at June, and June looked away. Silently Kerry shuffled into a bench by herself. Humiliation burned in her. She felt just the same way as she had in the days, which already seemed a long time ago, when Billy and his mob had waited for her after school. Why should June suddenly turn against her? She thought they were best friends. All through the lesson Kerry stared out of the window, first struggling to stem tears which threatened to spill out, and then trying to stop the anger which replaced the tears from escaping into her mouth and out again in a scream of rage. Things were going so well. She had just begun to feel safe again. Now this.

Ron Watts, aware that there was something going on, tactfully ignored the inattention of this usually hard-working pupil. When the bell went he asked June and Kerry to stay behind to collect the textbooks and put them back into the cupboard. Then he made a quick exit into the prep room just off the lab, hoping the two would sort themselves out.

June and Kerry stood at the front of the class and took the textbooks from the pupils filing out. 'I'll wait for you in the cloakroom,' said Susie to June. 'I'll get all your stuff together for you.'

'Yeah, thanks,' said June miserably. She was still not looking at Kerry.

'Are you walking home with Susie, then?' asked Kerry evenly. June and Kerry always walked home together; Susie lived a long way from the school, and only a small part of her route coincided with June and Kerry's.

'Yes,' said June.

They moved to the cupboard and started to pile the books on to the shelf.

'June, what have I done?' said Kerry at last, unable to bear the ice between them any more.

'Nothing,' said June.

'Oh, come on, I'm not thick. You're angry with me, and I can't see why. I thought we were best friends. Aren't we, any more?'

June shrugged. 'I thought so. But that was before Billy Taggart started following you around.'

'Billy Taggart?' Kerry was astonished, and then burst out laughing. 'For heaven's sake, you don't believe I fancy him, do you? Billy Taggart? I hope never to be that desperate.'

'No, I don't believe you fancy him,' said June. 'But there's obviously something going on between you, and whatever it is, it's not nice.'

'But what does that have to do with us?' asked Kerry, mystified at the troubled expression on June's face.

'Can't you see?' said June. She flushed a deep

red and faced Kerry squarely. June was a very easy-going girl and hated to make trouble. But she could not keep it inside any longer. 'Firstly, you are keeping secrets from me. Best friends are not supposed to do that. But also – the way you treat Billy is horrible. You look at him as though he's an insect, and you push him around. And he doesn't fight back. I don't know why he takes it. You've got power over him for some reason, and you're using it. I . . . I don't like to think a friend of mine could do that to someone.'

Having said her piece, June looked near to tears. She turned to leave, but Kerry caught her arm.

'You feel sorry for him, don't you? You actually feel sorry for Billy Taggart? How could you? He's a thug, and a bully . . . .'

'He's never done me any harm,' put in June quietly.

Kerry decided that she would have to tell June about the bullying. But not here, in this impersonal classroom, where anyone could overhear them.

'June, will you come round tonight, after tea? I'll tell you all about it then, I promise. You're right, I shouldn't keep secrets. When I've told you, you'll understand why Billy Taggart isn't worth feeling sorry for.'

'I've got to look after my sister tonight,' said June. She didn't seem convinced that Kerry could persuade her to think differently.

'Please,' said Kerry. 'Bring her with you. My mum and dad would love to have a little kid around – they'll play with her while we talk. Please, June.'

'All right,' said June. 'But I'm still walking home with Susie – she's waiting for me now.'

Kerry nodded. 'Yeah, OK. I'll see you tonight, then.'

"bye,' said June awkwardly, and was gone.

Thoughtfully, Kerry closed the cupboard door and snapped the lock shut. For the first time, she saw herself as June must have been seeing her these last few days – almost a bully herself. But when she had explained it all to June, everything would be all right again, she was sure. She was struck by a new wave of irritation. Billy Taggart was still managing to cause trouble for her, even now the bullying had stopped.

She turned to leave the room – and found Wayne standing in the doorway. She gave a little gasp, and automatically looked over her shoulder.

'He ain't here,' said Wayne. 'He's cleared off. It's just you and me, sweetheart.'

Kerry approached him with her heart thumping, but pretending to be cool. 'Get out of my way,' she said.

Wayne stood up straight in the doorway, completely blocking her path.

'Make me,' he said.

'I wouldn't soil my hands,' Kerry said, and swore silently at the tremor which she heard in her voice.

'No, that's right. You'll get Billy to do the dirty work, will you? You reckon what you've got on him is so strong he'll even beat me up? Oh, I think you should be very careful about that one, my little crippled friend. Billy isn't like that.'

'Well, are you going to let me past, or shall we put it to the test?' said Kerry.

Wayne pushed his face close to Kerry. She could feel his breath, hot and sour, and smoky. She could see the little red veins in the whites of his eyes, and small flakes of dandruff on his cheekbones. In spite of herself, she took a step back. Wayne smiled.

'I just want you to know,' he said, 'that I don't give a toss about you and Billy, and I'm gonna get you. Not here, and not now – that would be too easy. But one day, I'm gonna be waiting for you, Spas. And you won't know when, and you won't know what I'm going to do. You're gonna feel just like poor daft old Billy does now – only worse, because when I do get you, it's gonna really hurt. Now why don't you run to Billy and tell him that?' Wayne suddenly stood aside from the doorway, making Kerry flinch. He swept his arm low in front of him, with a mocking bow. She was forced to sidle past him, like a crab, not sure if he would actually let her go. Kerry felt once again the old fear, the old humiliation, of being someone's victim.

A swing door at the end of the corridor creaked. It was Billy, looking for Wayne. When he saw the two of them together, he stopped. Wayne looked at Kerry, his quick brown eyes daring her to tell Billy about his threats, daring her to force Billy to choose between them.

'Ah, there you are, Billy,' she said. 'Hello.'

Billy came up to them, silently and with a flush of shame. Did he think Kerry had told Wayne his secret? And why should Wayne care if Billy's dad was in prison, anyway? She couldn't work that one out, although she would use it as long as she could. 'Billy, would you do something for me?'

She looked at Wayne. For one glorious, breath-taking second she saw his confident smile falter. For just one instant he was unsure, scared.

'Billy, I've got loads of homework tonight and my bag's really heavy. Would you walk me home, please? You can carry my bag and – and make sure I'm not pestered by anybody on the way.'

Wayne glared at Billy as he took Kerry's bag and shuffled off down the corridor. He stopped at the door and looked round, waiting for Kerry to catch up. Kerry smiled at Wayne and Wayne growled with disgust and loped off in the opposite direction.

'Shaw!' they heard the headmaster bellowing from the other end of the corridor. Wayne would be occupied for a while now.

Kerry turned to Billy. He looked like a dog wearing a muzzle, a dog who would leap at her throat, given half a chance. She must be careful. What if he suddenly decided he had had enough? He would make her suffer for the power she had held over him. It would be ten times worse than the original bullying. Also, Wayne was probably right. Billy would not hurt his friend to save himself. That made Wayne dangerous, even if Billy could be controlled. It was enough to make her head ache just thinking about it all.

Kerry was also feeling a bit guilty. True, Billy deserved everything he was getting, but June had begun to turn against her. Billy's protection was not worth losing June for. Kerry just hoped June would show up that evening, and that Kerry's explanation would make her understand.

Billy was watching her. She turned away from his cold stare.

'Come on, then,' she said frostily. 'But don't walk beside me.'

'Who said I wanted to?' he sneered.

As they set off, Kerry realized that she no longer felt any thrill at all from having Billy in her power. She was beginning to feel afraid again.

5

Billy followed Kerry in silence, all the way home. Through the school gates, down the road, into the park and across to the back gate of Kerry's house, he walked a little way behind her, without saying a word. Kerry could feel his eyes boring into her back, willing her to drop dead. It was like a cold wave from the sea, Billy's hatred and humiliation. Kerry was also very conscious of her limp, and realized that having Billy walking behind her just made this worse. He could stare at her leg all he liked. She concentrated very hard on walking straight, but all in all it was a miserable journey.

Outside Kerry's garden gate, she turned and held out her hand for the bag. Billy scowled, and almost threw it at her; Kerry reeled a little from the weight of it. 'Thank you, Billy.' She smiled sweetly at him.

Billy stepped towards her and thrust his face near hers. 'Just watch it,' he said. 'I've been thinking. Being your slave is probably worse than having everyone find out about my dad. So lay off.'

Kerry considered. What June had said about the way she treated Billy was still fresh in her mind. Had he suffered enough for what he had done in the early days? Or should she keep him dangling? There was precious little fun left in it, suddenly.

'Tell you what,' she said. 'You just make sure I don't get hassled by your mob – or anyone else – and I'll leave you alone. And I won't tell, as long as I'm left alone.'

Billy's relief was obvious from the expression on his face. Kerry even saw the word 'thanks' being framed on his lips, but he recalled it in time.

'It's a deal,' he said. He turned to slope off, but the sound of someone banging on the window drew their attention.

Kerry's mum leaned out of the window upstairs. 'Wait a minute!' she called, and disappeared.

Uncertain and uneasy, Billy shuffled his feet. He looked at Kerry, a question in his eyes.

'Get going,' said Kerry.

Billy turned, and had managed to cover some distance before the garden gate was wrenched open by Kerry's mother. Unfortunately, he could not pretend to be out of earshot.

'Young man!' she called.

Billy turned, reluctantly, and slowly walked back to Kerry and her mother. Kerry saw her mother smiling indulgently at him, and was gripped with horror as she realized that her mother thought Kerry and Billy were friends. As she met Billy's eyes she saw the same idea had occurred to him, and he felt just as she did about it.

'Hello,' said Kerry's mum, and held out her hand. 'I'm Liz Hollis, Kerry's mum.'

Kerry had always liked the way her mum treated children as though they were quite grown-up, but

50

her skin crawled with embarrassment now. Billy, confused, looked at the outstretched hand and didn't quite know what to do. Finally he touched it, briefly, with his own. There was a bright red spot on each cheek. 'Billy Taggart,' he said briefly.

'It's so kind of you to help Kerry with her bag,' said Liz Hollis. 'I'm happy to see Kerry has found another friend at school.'

Billy didn't answer.

Kerry's mum looked at him for a moment with a faintly puzzled air. He did not look like the sort of boy she would expect to befriend Kerry. But, for all her failings, Liz Hollis was no snob. If he was a friend of her daughter's, that was good enough for her.

'Do you like chocolate cake?' she asked suddenly.

Billy, suspicious of the question, muttered, 'It's all right.'

'I've just made one,' said Kerry's mum. She laughed. 'It seems to be the way to meet Kerry's friends – last time I made chocolate cake a friend of Kerry's appeared, and now you're here. Come along inside and have some tea with us.'

Before Billy and Kerry knew what was happening, she had ushered them halfway down the path towards the house.

Billy came to his senses, and wailed, 'I got to get home.'

'Nonsense.' Mrs Hollis, once gripped by an idea, was not a woman to be stopped. She took Billy's arm, and guided him through the conservatory and into the living room. 'Can I take your coat?' she asked pleasantly. Billy, whose mouth was hanging

51

open as he looked around him, seemed rooted to the spot. Mrs Hollis pulled his coat from his shoulders and took it out to the hall. Billy shifted his feet uneasily in the deep, cream-coloured carpet. He looked down at his shoes.

They were dull plastic, smeared with old mud from football games on the school field. There were cracks across the toes. He seemed to be looking at them for the first time, as though he had never noticed them before. Kerry had to admit that Billy looked very out of place in her house. He was always grubby and unkempt, but here amid the leather sofas, the deep carpet and the shining glass he looked like a stray picked up from a Victorian street.

'Sit down, Billy,' she said. 'Once my mum's got an idea, there's no arguing with her. Just have your cake and go.'

Billy sat gingerly on the edge of the sofa. Automatically, he tried to tuck his feet under it, out of sight, but the sofa reached down to the floor. His eyes were rooted to the spot on the carpet where he had stood. A piece of dried mud had fallen off on to it. The little cake of mud lay on the carpet, surrounded by crumbs which had flaked from it when it fell off his shoe. For a moment, Kerry actually felt sorry for him, sharing his embarrassment. Swiftly, she picked up the piece of mud and tossed it into the bin on the other side of the room. Billy was clearly impressed by her aim. His eyes travelled round the room again, noting the velvet curtains, the television and video, the compact-disc player and the red leather and gold bindings on the books which filled the shelves.

Kerry's mother returned with a tray, which she placed on the coffee table near to Billy. His eyes moved to the chocolate cake, and his tongue moved over his lower lip. Kerry wondered what Billy's own home was like. Did his mother ever make chocolate cake for him? She thought not.

Mrs Hollis was cutting a generous slice and placing it on a delicate china plate. She held it out to Billy. 'There you are.'

Billy reached out for the plate. Kerry saw that his hands, like the rest of him, were rather grubby, and his bitten nails had black lines across them.

Her mother, however, did not seem to notice. 'If someone's expecting you home,' she said to Billy. 'You can telephone, if you like.'

Billy shook his head.

'That's all right, then.' Mrs Hollis settled back on to the sofa, next to Kerry. She looked from her daughter to Billy, and back. Again the puzzled look crossed her face. They were certainly an odd couple. The poor lad was obviously very nervous; he seemed terrified he would break something, perched on the sofa like an overgrown budgie in a small cage, waiting for release. The chocolate cake lay untouched on his plate. For the first time it occurred to her that actually neither the boy nor her daughter had wanted her to make this gesture of friendship with the chocolate cake. But it was too late now, so she soldiered on.

'Tea?' she asked. Billy looked at the impossibly fragile cups, covered with tiny roses, settling on their paper-thin saucers. Miserably, he shook his head. 'No – thank you,' he added hurriedly.

Mrs Hollis looked at Kerry, who was staring down at the carpet and trying not to laugh. 'Right. Um, well, look – I'll just leave the tray here, all right? You can help yourselves as and when. I've, um, got to finish the Hoovering upstairs.'

She left the room. Kerry, who had noted the third cup and saucer on the tray, breathed a sigh of relief. At least they were going to be spared the ordeal of her mother's conversation.

'Don't you like cake?' she asked Billy. Her voice sounded almost kind. Billy, a little more relaxed now that Mrs Hollis had left, nodded, and took a bite. He ate carefully, putting his hand to his mouth as though to hide it. Kerry tactfully looked away out of the window while she took a bite from her own slice.

There was a long silence. They both chewed their cake automatically, wondering how quickly they could bring this farce to a close. Billy broke the silence. 'It's lovely,' he said. 'Your mum's cake.'

This little piece of polite conversation took Kerry by surprise. It was as though the elegant surroundings had forced the two of them into a pattern of polite behaviour, like guests at a tea party.

'Yes,' she said. 'All my mum's cakes are good, but chocolate is my favourite.'

There was another silence. 'Would you like another piece?' she asked.

Billy looked longingly at the cake. 'No, better not,' he said.

Kerry smiled. 'Will your mum be cross if you spoil your tea at home?' she teased.

A shadow crossed Billy's face. 'No. I'm getting the tea tonight, anyway,' he said.

'I didn't know you could cook,' said Kerry.

Billy shrugged. He did not want to continue the conversation.

'Tell you what,' said Kerry. 'I'll give you some to take home.' She laughed. There was something weird about this situation. Here she was chatting with a thug and a bully over tea and cake as if they were old neighbours.

Billy scowled. 'I don't want your bleedin' charity.'

'I didn't mean . . . I wasn't laughing at you!' said Kerry.

'No, 'course you weren't,' said Billy. His voice was hard and bitter. 'Just little Lady Bountiful, with money oozing out of her, being nice to the local peasant. Now look 'ere, Hollis. I ain't ashamed of not 'aving a phone, nor fancy carpets, nor a mum who's got nothin' better to do than make cakes for a spoilt bitch of a kid. I didn't want to stay, and I didn't want your bleedin' cake, neither. You think you're clever, don't you, shoving me around all the time? Fair enough – you got somethin' on me, and I 'ave to pay the price. But just don't make that price too high, if you're smart.'

Kerry was astonished. It was the longest speech she had heard Billy make, and it mirrored almost exactly what she herself had been thinking.

'Billy, I wasn't being Lady Bountiful. I was just offering you some cake. And I've told you, just keep your mob off me and we'll be quits. I don't want

55

any more to do with you, as long as you make sure *I'm* left alone.'

Billy snarled at her, and then gave a slight nod. He got to his feet. Chocolate crumbs dropped to the carpet. 'I'm going now,' he said.

Kerry led Billy to the hall and let him out through the front door. At the little wrought-iron gate which led on to the street, he turned. 'Tell your mum goodbye,' he said unexpectedly. 'And tell her thanks for the cake'.

Kerry slammed the door and heaved a big sigh of relief. She wandered into the living room and picked up the tray, to carry through to the kitchen.

'Has Billy gone, then?' her mother called from the top of the stairs. Kerry watched her mother as she struggled down the stairs with the Hoover. 'You've never mentioned him before, Kerry. You dark horse, you.'

'Mum, he's not . . . we're just . . . .'

'Just good friends. Say no more.' Her mother winked at her. 'He seems a nice lad – very shy, poor thing.'

Kerry almost laughed aloud. Billy Taggart, shy? Then she remembered his face as he entered the living room, the shuffling feet, the red cheeks. Yes, he was shy.

'He said thanks for the cake,' she said.

'He doesn't look as though he gets much chocolate cake, does he?' said her mother. 'Do you know anything about his family?'

'No,' Kerry lied.

'Mmm. My guess would be it's best not to ask,' said her mother.

Kerry's heart filled with love for her mother, with her anxious face and her hair already sprinkled with grey. She had been so good at dealing with people once, bright and confident and assertive. She had been in charge of the personnel office for a large company, and her days had been full of drama and intrigue as she tried to sort out the problems of the staff there, to keep them happy at work.

After the accident she had given it all up, saying that nearly losing Kerry had made her realize how short those years of Kerry's childhood were. She had reassessed her priorities, she'd said. It had been a while before Kerry had understood what these words meant, but she had known they had something to do with having her mother at home every day after school, and home-baked cakes, and more time for doing things together. She had been happy to have her mother all to herself.

Now Kerry began to realize how self-centred and childish that was. ' . . . nothing better to do with her time than make cakes for a spoiled bitch of a kid . . . .' Was Kerry a spoiled bitch? She didn't feel like one – but then, she wouldn't, would she?

Her mother must surely miss all the bustle and people at work. She never said anything, but Kerry knew running a house did not give her mother the same satisfaction that being at work had done. That was why she was too involved in Kerry's life, too worried about everything. She had nothing else to think about.

'Mum, don't you ever think about going back to work?' she asked.

Her mother was taken by surprise. 'What a question. Why do you ask?'

Kerry frowned. 'You must get bored, here all day by yourself.'

'I find plenty to do, don't worry. Of course I miss work sometimes, but I've never regretted giving up. You and your father are much more important.' She opened the cupboard door in the kitchen and pushed the Hoover in. 'When you're older I might consider going back,' she said. 'Perhaps part-time, at first, and then . . . well, we'll see.'

'I'm older now,' said Kerry. 'I'm capable of looking after myself, mostly.'

Mrs Hollis hugged her daughter and held her at arm's length, studying her. 'Yes, you certainly are growing up,' she said. She laughed. 'You must bring that young man home properly one day, when your father's here, so that we can find out if his intentions are honourable.'

'Oh, Mum!' Kerry threw a tea towel at her mother.

Going back into the living room, Kerry looked at the little patch of mud and chocolate crumbs. For the first time, she wondered what sort of life Billy led. Was he really as hard as he made himself out to be when he was with Wayne?

Wayne. A picture of his face burned itself into her mind, the little malicious eyes glowing. 'I'll get you!' he had said.

Kerry would rather have Billy's open bullying than the sort of thing a mind like Wayne's might dream up. She shivered.

6

June appeared that evening as promised, with little Rosie in tow. Rosie was just six, and lived up to her name. She would have looked exactly like June except that she had inherited her father's very dark hair and round red cheeks, while June had the light hair and pale complexion of her mother. Kerry's father laughed about this when he saw them together. 'You look like an advertisement,' he said. 'Here we have our latest model in young girls, available in two delightful colour schemes.'

Kerry groaned, but little Rosie giggled and June smiled politely.

'Well now, Rosie, Kerry's mummy and I were just about to start a game of tiddleywinks and we were wondering who on earth we could ask to play with us, because everybody knows you have to have three to make a proper game of it. Do you have any idea who we could ask?'

Rosie slipped her hand into her big sister's and tugged it. 'Rosie knows how to play tiddleywinks,' said June.

'Do you really?' Kerry's dad pretended to be

astonished. 'Would you like to play with us, little Rosie?'

Rosie nodded.

'Come on, then – let's go and find Kerry's mummy.' He held out his hand, and Rosie took it and allowed herself to be led into the kitchen.

'Thanks, Dad,' said Kerry.

He smiled over his shoulder. 'Believe me, I'd rather play tiddleywinks any day than have to listen to two giggling females of the teenage variety discussing the merits and failings of the entire male population of Southside Comprehensive'.

'Your dad's great with kids, isn't he?' said June as the girls settled themselves on to Kerry's bed and turned the radio on. 'Why did your parents only have one?'

'I don't know, really,' said Kerry. 'I know they wanted more. My mum had at least two miscarriages, maybe more. I suppose they just gave up trying, or perhaps they just never managed to have another one. I don't know.'

'Haven't you asked?' said June, surprised.

'No, of course not,' said Kerry, equally surprised that June should ask the question.

'Blimey, I would,' said June.

'It's not really my business,' said Kerry. 'And it might be painful for them to talk about it. They never ask me questions about painful things – they wait for me to tell them, if I want to. So I do the same.'

'Very civilized,' said June. 'In my family, everybody is thoroughly questioned about everything, from what they had for lunch down to what they

60

think might happen in a nuclear war. We can almost read each other's thoughts.'

Kerry was not sure she would like that. 'Mmm,' she said, thinking it best not to comment.

They listened in companionable silence to the music. Then a record neither of them particularly liked came on.

'Right,' said June. 'Tell me what's going on between you and Billy. I've been dying to know.'

Kerry told her about the bullying, and June's eyes grew wide. Bullying, in June's book, was not something you kept quiet about, and it wasn't covered by the usual rules about snitching on someone. If she was bullied by a lout like Taggart she would be outside the Head's office so fast he would hardly have a chance to lower his fist. Bullies didn't deserve protection. Surely a sensible girl like Kerry could see that. And yet she had taken it all, for weeks, without saying a word to anyone. June couldn't understand that, but then June had never been bullied. So she bit back the question she wanted to ask, which was why Kerry had allowed it to happen more than once, and just nodded to encourage Kerry to go on with the story.

Kerry hesitated when she got to the part about reading the newspaper and finding out about Billy's dad. 'I promised I wouldn't tell anybody,' she said. 'You must promise you'll never let anyone know.'

June promised, of course, and Kerry told her. June wanted to see the story for herself, and again Kerry hesitated. 'It's in a suitcase under my bed,' she said. June waited expectantly. 'Look, June, there's something else I've got to tell you – another secret. You promise it'll stay between us, no one else?'

Again, June nodded. Kerry pulled out the suitcase, and opened it. She placed one of the silver trophies in June's lap. June read the inscription, and gave a little gasp. She looked at Kerry's leg, and then up at Kerry's flaming face. Without saying anything, Kerry put the scrapbook on her friend's lap, and June looked through it. Pictures of Kerry, crippled Kerry, flying through the air, arcing over a high bar, kicking her now mangled leg high and straight, arms outstretched, face bright and confident. Then the final story, of a young gymnast withdrawing from the national team after a tragic accident which ended her hopes of an Olympic medal. No picture, just one small cutting at the end of the scrapbook. June felt herself close to tears. Poor Kerry. How could she bear it? June didn't know what to say. In Kerry's family hurt like this was papered over, no one seemed to share it. She sensed that Kerry's accident was not something to be talked about, and with an effort she put the book down and said nothing except, 'Oh, Kerry.'

Kerry brushed a tear from her own eye briskly and said, 'Yes, well now you know. But this is what I really wanted to show you.'

She turned the newspaper to the piece about William Taggart, of Bracknell Street, Burfield, sentenced to fifteen years' imprisonment for a series of assaults and robberies in the homes of defenceless elderly women. Taggart was a married man, with a young son, and the judge had commented on the cold-blooded way Taggart had used him to call on

the women prior to his crimes – saying the little
boy needed a drink of water, so that he could look
around. The boy was not named. The judge said
that although the boy had agreed to go along with
the deception, he could not have had any idea why
his father wanted to see inside the old ladies' houses,
and it was likely he was forced into obeying his
father with threats of strong punishment.

June gave a low whistle. 'What a find,' she said.
'What did Billy say, when you showed him?'

'Well,' said Kerry, 'I wasn't absolutely sure it
was the same family, although the name seemed a
bit of a coincidence and I had heard somewhere
that Taggart had moved here from up north. But
when I mentioned it he almost wet himself, so I
knew it was the same family, all right. That's when
Billy and I made our little agreement.' She grinned.
'Much to Wayne's disgust, of course.'

'What I can't understand,' said June thoughtfully, 'is why Billy didn't just tell Wayne. They're
best friends – Wayne would keep it quiet. And even
if he did tell everyone, why should Billy Taggart
care? Everyone knows he's a thug, and to find out
his father is one as well wouldn't surprise anybody.'

'I've been wondering that myself,' said Kerry. 'I
don't know. But I've seen on the telly how even
criminals turn against people who've hurt children
or old people. It's so disgusting, maybe even Wayne
would turn against Billy.'

'But it wasn't Billy's fault, was it?
Unless . . . unless Billy did know what his father
was up to, all along. Let's see, he must have been
about –' June looked at the article to see when

the crimes had been committed, and did a quick calculation from the date on the paper – 'about eight. Quite old enough to understand, if his dad chose to tell him. Mind you, he's very slow on the uptake even now, isn't he? What a creep his dad must have been.'

'Well, it's all been a stroke of luck for me,' said Kerry. 'None of his gang have laid a finger on me since I found it.'

'It can't go on, though.' June folded the paper neatly and handed it back with the scrapbook for Kerry to put away. 'Wayne is not thick. He must have worked out that you've got something on Billy. Pretty soon he'll work out a way to find out what's going on. Meanwhile, if you seem to be going too far with Billy it might just be worth his while to come after you himself, and deal with Billy afterwards.'

'I think that's what he's got in mind,' said Kerry, and she told June what had happened after the maths lesson. She said nothing about Billy coming in for tea, however. That had been a different Billy, a shy and uncomfortable boy. Kerry did not want to admit that she could have anything to do with Taggart the bully, the criminal's son who had helped his father set up attacks on old people.

'You'll just have to be careful,' said June finally. 'You say you've told Billy you'll lay off him as long as you're not bullied any more. Maybe that will be enough. I doubt it, though. Even in the infants, Wayne was never one to let anybody score a point off him.'

The bedroom door opened and Rosie danced in, with her cheeks bulging.

'What have you got?' asked June indulgently.

Rosie promptly opened her mouth to show a churning mass of chocolate, toffee and saliva. 'Sweety,' she said, and a little brown stream escaped from her mouth and tracked its way towards her chin.

Both Kerry and June made disgusted noises. 'Aw, Rosie!' said June.

Rosie wiped her chin with her hand, and finished her sweet purposefully. She had a message to deliver. 'Kerry's daddy says he is tiddleywinked to the eyeballs and wants to read the paper,' she said, proud that she had remembered the message exactly.

'I've got to go, anyway,' said June. 'It's my turn to wash up tonight, and Dad will be wanting to bath Rosie and get her to bed before his telly programme comes on. Right then, little Rosie, let's be off.'

Rosie gave Kerry a sticky kiss somewhere between the chin and the cheek and obediently followed her big sister down the stairs and into the hall, where Kerry's mum was waiting to say goodbye. She put little Rosie's coat on, and gave her a hug. Kerry, watching from the landing, felt sad for her mother, for both her parents. They loved children so much, and yet had only one of their own. And that one precious child had not even stayed healthy and whole.

Billy was the only child at home, since his brother was in the Army. But Wayne Shaw had a whole tribe of brothers and sisters, one in almost every year at the school and a couple waiting to come up from the juniors. They all looked alike and cared for nobody, not even the people in their own family. They never walked to school together or took any notice of each other once they got there. No one ever saw their parents. It was not fair. Kerry would have loved to have been a big sister, like June, who was clasping Rosie's little hand and smiling down at her sticky face.

"bye, then,' said June. Rosie gave a little wave, and Kerry's mother saw them out to the street. Kerry went into her bedroom, to wave from the window. June waved back, and pointed up to show Rosie, who smiled and waved too. Then they went off down the road. Kerry heard her mother shut the front door. She was just about to turn away from the window when her eye was caught by a slight movement on the other side of the road. It was almost dark, and the tree on the other side seemed to have something attached to its trunk, although Kerry could not see what it was. Then it moved. Wayne stepped away from the tree, where he had been hiding while June and Rosie left. He looked up at Kerry's window, and pointed his finger straight up at her. 'Got you!' it seemed to say. She stared at him, feeling her heart begin to thump, and then she pulled the curtain. When she looked again, he had gone. Or perhaps he was hiding behind the tree, or in her garden somewhere. How could she tell?

Kerry sank on to her bed and pulled her old teddy into her arms, hugging it close. Wayne had wanted to frighten her, and he had succeeded. The bullying was starting again.

7

The first thing Kerry did when she woke up the next morning was pull back the curtains and look out at the tree opposite her house. Although she could hardly believe Wayne would have stayed there all night, she still breathed a sigh of relief when she could find no sign of him on the street.

June came to call for Kerry, as usual, and knew something was wrong as soon as they left Kerry's driveway. It was pouring with rain, 'coming down like stair rods', as June put it, and so they could not go across the park. Kerry kept looking over her shoulder, as though she expected to see someone behind her. The umbrella they were sharing offered little protection from the rain when the person holding it kept swivelling around and lifting it up to see past it.

'For heaven's sake, Kerry, what's the matter?'

'Wayne was outside the house when you left last night. Did you see him?'

'No. What was he doing?'

'He was just leaning against the tree, watching. When he saw me, he kind of leered, and pointed at me.'

'Pointed at you?' echoed June. 'What for?'

'I'm not sure, really. I think he just wanted to give me a scare; you know, let me see that he was watching, and could get me any time he wanted.' Kerry looked over her shoulder again.

June, ducking so as not to be swiped by the umbrella swinging round on her, said, 'Well he's certainly succeeded in frightening you, hasn't he? What do you think he's going to do to you, Kerry, out here on the street in broad daylight?'

'Nothing,' admitted Kerry. 'I know he couldn't do anything. But that's not how bullying works, is it? You don't have to beat the person up, not every day. Just him being around is enough to scare me, because of what I know he *could* do.'

June considered this, and shook her head. 'I can't see that there's anything to worry about,' she said. 'He may try to frighten you, but he can't actually do anything. Billy would make mincemeat of him in a fight. Anyway, if he lays a finger on you, go to the Head. Wayne's a little creep, and you can't let him get away with it.'

'It's humiliating enough being the one who's picked on,' said Kerry, 'without running to a teacher and asking to be looked after like an infant.'

'You only need to tell someone once, and he'll leave you alone. How many other kids is that little mob having a go at, that you and I don't know about? Why should they be allowed to pick on anyone they choose and make their lives miserable? If they laid a finger on me, believe me, I would split on them to anyone and everyone.'

Kerry simply shrugged. 'Maybe you're just

braver than me,' she said. 'Maybe I shouldn't have told you about it.' Her face was obstinate.

June sighed, and decided to drop the subject. Bullies chose their victims carefully, she thought, and her own views that shopping a bully to the teachers was a good thing to do, not like ordinary snitching on someone, was probably what saved her from being picked on in the first place.

'Besides, what could the Head do?' said Kerry. 'Wayne was standing outside my house. He *pointed* at me. Big crime, eh? And he and Billy used to get at me in the park – even if I could prove it, which would be almost impossible since I've covered it up right from the start, I can't claim they're hurting me now, can I? It's all finished, and Billy has turned over a new leaf. That's how the Head will see it, particularly if I didn't tell him about seeing the bit in the paper and using it to get Billy's protection – and I could hardly do that, now could I?'

She was right, June could see that. What a mess. All June could do was stay close to Kerry and wait for the storm to blow over. Wayne would get fed up in the end, and move on to someone who was an easier target. Maybe.

The two girls trailed miserably together to school. There was no sign of Wayne or Billy. Fats sidled past them in the corridor without looking at them. This probably meant that both Wayne and Billy were absent from school, and Fats was avoiding anyone who might take the opportunity of getting even with the mob through him. Where were they? What were they planning? Had Billy told Wayne his secret? If so, they were probably working out something really nasty to pay Kerry back for trying to split them up. All morning her imagination ran riot. She could pay no attention to the lessons, and was told off several times for daydreaming. In French, she was even called out to the front and made to answer the questions on the board, with the teacher's chalk.

'At least, that way I can see you are actually taking some notice of what's going on in the lesson,' said Miss Craig grimly. 'I see Master Taggart is not in school today – are you going to moon around like this until he comes back, Kerry? I wish you girls would learn not to let your love lives interfere with your work.'

The class roared with laughter, and Kerry's face burned. She answered the questions and sat down. For the first time, she began to believe that June was right, that she should have told someone after the very first time Wayne and Billy and Fats had waited for her in the park. In the end, it would have been simpler. She would have felt humiliated, having to ask a teacher for protection, but being looked upon as Billy Taggart's girlfriend was far worse. It was too late now, though. She would have to find another way out.

As June and Kerry passed the park gates on the way home that night, Wayne was waiting. It was raining again, and his thin jacket was plastered to his skin. His dark hair clung to his scalp, and his eyes squinted against the little streams of rainwater which kept dripping off on to his face.

'Hello, Kerry. Hello, June. How are you keeping?' he called. 'What awful weather we're having. Hope to see you tonight, Kerry.' He winked at her.

'Shove off!' said June.

Wayne laughed, and watched them walk on down the road.

'He must be planning something for tonight,' said Kerry. She shivered, feeling the rain seeping into her bones and washing the fear around them until they turned to jelly. 'What do you think he's going to do?'

'Nothing,' said June. 'Maybe he'll just prop up that old tree again – stay indoors and don't look out of the window, and you won't give him the satisfaction.'

Kerry didn't answer; when June looked at her, she saw that her face was white. 'What's up?' she asked.

'Dad's working late tonight,' she said. 'He won't be back until about nine. Mum's cookery class down at the evening institute starts at seven-thirty.'

'Wayne can't know that, though – can he?'

'What if he does?' said Kerry.

'I'll come over,' said June promptly. 'I'll be there about seven, and I won't leave until your dad gets in.'

'Thanks, June. I'm glad I told you about it all; it really helps to have someone who knows. You were right, though. I should have told someone – teachers, or Dad, someone like that – right at the start. This is so ridiculous. I'm even scared to stay in my own house for an hour by myself.'

'We must find out what the situation is with Billy,' said June. 'We must know whether you can still count on him, or whether Wayne knows about his dad. I wonder why Billy wasn't with Wayne? They often skive off school together to go fishing, but maybe it was just coincidence that they were both off today.'

'If he's off again tomorrow, maybe we can ask his form teacher if there's been a note or something,' said Kerry. 'When someone plays truant as often as Billy, they usually insist on a note after the first day, don't they?'

'You can ask,' laughed June. 'It will be quite in keeping with the popular idea that you're missing him so badly.' She mimicked Miss Craig. 'I really do wish you girls would learn to keep your love lives separate from your school work, Kerry Hollis. What do you see in a boy like Billy Taggart?'

'Oh, Miss Craig,' breathed Kerry with an exaggerated expression of hero worship. 'He's so strong and powerful – a real man!' For the first time, Kerry found herself laughing about the mess she was in.

June came over that evening as promised, but there was no sign of Wayne. They drew the living-room curtains and peeped out from behind them at regular intervals, but could not see him. Just before nine, Kerry's dad arrived home. He looked very tired, but his face brightened when he saw the two girls. 'More girl talk?' he teased. 'Come on then, what's the latest? Who fancies whom, and what are they going to do about it?'

'Oh, Dad, shut up,' groaned Kerry. 'Shall I make you some tea?'

'Tea! Oh yes, a cup of tea would be great,' said Dad. 'You must come over more often, June. Kerry clearly wants to impress you with her dutiful daughterliness. It usually takes a huge bribe, or threat of physical punishment, to get a cup of tea out of Kerry.'

June smiled. Kerry threw a cushion, which her father caught and threw back at her. 'By the way,' he said, 'I have a message from one of your admirers.'

'What?' said Kerry. Her heart started to thump. 'Who?'

'Little weaselly chap with dark hair – not quite your type, I would have thought, but there's no accounting for taste. I met him up the road.'

'Wayne,' said June.

'Yes, I believe that was his name. Anyway, he says he's sorry he couldn't make it tonight, but he'll be sure to see you tomorrow after school. Billy can't come, whatever that might mean.'

Kerry's father lay back against the armchair and closed his eyes. 'Go and put the kettle on then,' he said. He did not notice the sudden silence or the tense look on his daughter's face.

'Tell him,' mouthed June. 'Tell him the truth.'

Kerry shook her head. 'Not now,' she mouthed back. 'Later – maybe later.'

June opened her mouth to say something else, but quickly closed it when she noticed that Kerry's dad had one eye open, looking at her.

'Today, if possible,' said Kerry's dad.

'Er . . . pardon, Dad?'

'The tea, Kerry. I would be grateful if you could make it today – as in *now*.'

'Ah, yes. Sorry, Dad. I'm on my way.'

'Kerry, you could have told your dad about Wayne just then and got this whole mess sorted out,' hissed June as soon as they were in the kitchen. 'You just said you wished you'd told someone – well, now's your chance. Go on!'

'No, he's too tired,' said Kerry. 'He's had a busy day, and now isn't the time.'

'You just don't want to,' said June scornfully. 'You know as well as I do that you won't say anything once your mum gets back, because she'll get too upset.'

Kerry was surprised that June seemed to know what she was thinking. 'Your dad would know what to do,' said June. 'Go and get it off your chest.'

'You don't understand,' said Kerry.

'Oh, stop being such a wimp, Kerry. Look, you go and tell your dad, or I will.'

June made a move towards the door, but Kerry grabbed her arm. 'Don't you dare!' she said. 'And don't call me a wimp. It's easy for you, isn't it? It's not you that's been picked on, followed, kicked around like a ball, is it? You're not a cripple – a spas – and you don't understand what it's like. I was like you once. I would have looked at someone like me, someone being bullied, and I would have stopped it. But when you're the one on the receiving end, it's not so easy.' A tear trickled out of her eye and rolled down her cheek. June moved to comfort her, but Kerry brushed her friend aside and reached for the teapot.

'It is simple to stop it,' said June. 'Just tell.'

'Easy for you, isn't it?' said Kerry savagely. 'I'd just like to see what you would do if they waited for you after school one night. You're full of brave words now, but I bet you wouldn't find it so simple if it was you, in my place.'

'I would never be in your place,' said June, 'because I would never let it get this far. Look, Kerry I would feel sorry for you if you didn't already feel so sorry for yourself. They started the bullying, but you are the one who lets it carry on. You must either want it to carry on, or you're too proud – or too much of a wimp – to go for help.'

'Why don't you just stay out of it?' Kerry felt very bitter at what she thought was her friend's contempt for her. 'If I'm such a wimp, why bother sticking around? In fact, I'd prefer it if you just left me alone.'

June stared at her without answering for a moment. Then she said, 'Perhaps you deserve what Wayne's planning for you tomorrow. Just don't come to me for help – I've tried, but I've had enough!'

'June . . . .' Kerry turned to say she was sorry, but June was in the hall and striding through the front door. She slammed it behind her.

Kerry's dad appeared in the kitchen doorway. 'What about the tea then? Oh-oh,' he said when he saw Kerry's face. 'I thought the front door sounded a bit angry. You two have had a spat, have you?'

'A bit more than that,' said Kerry. 'Dad, will you make the tea? I want to go upstairs.'

Her father nodded understandingly. 'Go on, you look washed out. 'night.'

''night,' said Kerry. She knew she couldn't tell Dad anything; it would get back to Mum, and Mum would be crushed to think that her bright, energetic daughter could be reduced to such a jelly. She would blame herself; all the guilt about the accident would surface yet again. No, she would have to deal with this by herself. Or perhaps not quite by herself . . .

'Well, Billy Taggart,' Kerry murmured, 'looks like I'll have to lean on you again. Once and for all, Wayne Shaw has to be dealt with.'

8

The next morning, June walked past Kerry's house on the other side of the road, not even looking in the direction of Kerry, who stood hopefully at the front-room window. Kerry's heart sank. June was so easy-going, Kerry had hoped the quarrel would be forgotten, but it seemed not.

'You've gone too far this time, Kerry Hollis,' she muttered miserably to herself, and walked to school alone. She felt so miserable that she didn't even bother to try to walk straight. Her limp was more pronounced than usual, but she didn't care.

Wayne was talking to Fats near the entrance to the school grounds. Fats saw Kerry first and nudged Wayne, who turned and smiled. 'See you later, sweetheart,' he called, and waved. Kerry's face burned, but she pretended she had not heard. She had to find Billy today. If he would just make Wayne promise to leave her alone, she would let Billy off the hook for ever. She would start afresh. If anyone ever tried to bully her again, she would stand up to them, report it to the Head, do whatever she had to do. But first the slate had to be wiped clean with Wayne and Billy. She couldn't report either of them without the events of the past months coming out; they had to agree to leave her alone. Let them pick on someone else instead, she thought to herself – and then was immediately ashamed. What was she saying? How could she wish to inflict what she had been through, was still suffering, on another innocent victim? June was right. Kerry was a coward, pure and simple. She was becoming just like Fats.

As Kerry struggled up the steps to the front of the school, Mrs Tyson watched her thoughtfully. The child was beginning to look depressed again. She had seemed to be bouncing back, but her face this morning was telling another story entirely. Anyone who thought she had put the accident behind her and come to terms with the end of her gymnastics career had only to look at that pale face and dark shadowed eyes to see how wrong they were. An idea suddenly occurred to her, and she beckoned Kerry into a quiet corner of the old-fashioned quadrangle.

'Look,' she said briskly, 'I know you don't want to talk about what's happened to you, and I respect that. But you've been tearing yourself apart over it for long enough.'

How on earth had Mrs Tyson found out about Wayne and Billy? The answer came to Kerry in a flash. 'June!' she said bitterly. 'June's been talking to you, hasn't she? Well it's none of her business, and it's not true, anyway!'

Mrs Tyson looked confused for a moment, and then shook her head. 'I don't know what you're talking about Kerry, but I'm talking about your

79

accident, which you must know is on your school file. June hasn't told me anything.'

Kerry looked at her in surprise. So this was nothing to do with the bullies. She felt strangely disappointed, as though a door had been closed. To cover this, she adopted a very attentive expression.

'I can see why you don't want to come to the gym club,' said Mrs Tyson, 'but I think you would be surprised at how much you would be able to do, if you put your mind to it. I'm involved with a sports club for disabled people on a Monday evening. Some of them are in wheelchairs, some can only walk with two sticks, but you wouldn't believe the things they do: sailing, tennis, rock climbing, weightlifting . . . '

'You want me to join this club?' asked Kerry, trying not to sound sullen.

'No, Kerry. You're not really a disabled person – one day your leg will be all right again. As a matter of fact, most of the injury is inside your head now, not in your leg at all. I'm just trying to make you see that you don't have to be a perfect gymnast – you could lower your standards a bit and still get a lot from it. Now, the gym club meets in the second half of the dinner hour – take that mulish expression off your face, Kerry, I'm not suggesting you come along. The thing is, the lesson before lunch is a gymnastics lesson, and so the equipment is all left out. There's no one around for the first half of the lunch hour, no one at all.'

'I see,' said Kerry, as Mrs Tyson's idea began to dawn on her.

Mrs Tyson nodded enthusiastically. 'Normally,

of course, I would insist on someone being there if you were going to use the apparatus,' she said, 'but I'm only a shout away in the office, and you're a sensible, competent girl. What say you get your leotard on, and have a go? Work out your limitations, discover exactly what you can do, instead of mourning what you can't.'

'I can't do any of it,' said Kerry.

'Have you tried? I know you do quite a lot of physiotherapy, but have you actually worked out in a gym since the accident?'

'Of course not!' Kerry almost laughed, the idea seemed so absurd.

'How can you know then? Don't be so arrogant, Kerry. No one's going to pretend you'll ever compete again, but you can still do gymnastics – or was it only ever the prizes you were interested in?'

Kerry felt tears prick at her eyelids. 'No, not the prizes. It was – well, the power, I suppose. I was in control of my whole body, and I was beautiful – not pretty or anything, I don't mean it that way,' she added hastily. 'The movements were beautiful, and it was like being good at painting, or music . . . I can't really explain it,' she finished lamely.

'I think I understand,' said Mrs Tyson gently. 'I do, really, Kerry. You miss it all very much, don't you? But you could have all that again, you know. Look, think about it. Your PE kit is in school, isn't it? Well, then: if you want to use the gym at dinnertime, just go ahead. If you don't, that's fine by me – I've at least given you the chance. I won't talk about this again, or ask how it worked out. And all this will be just between you and me, OK?'

Kerry smiled at her. Here was just about the only teacher on earth who could actually understand what was going on in her head, and yet not try to interfere. She was giving Kerry the choice, and leaving it up to her.

'Thanks, Miss,' she said. Mrs Tyson smiled and walked away, leaving Kerry feeling a bit more cheerful, although she had no intention of going to the gym at dinnertime, not to use the apparatus, anyway. Maybe she could just go and have a look. At least it would take her mind off Wayne.

At registration Kerry smiled across at June, and June smiled back. When Kerry came to take her usual place next to June for the first lesson, history, June said nothing, but she didn't move away. Things were not completely back to normal between them, but at least it was a start.

Kerry anxiously scoured the school for Billy at break, but there was no sign of him. She saw Wayne again, with Fats in tow as usual. They were disappearing behind the cycle sheds, the favourite spot for smokers. Today being Wednesday, Mr Cartwright was on break duty, and everyone knew that he was scared of his own shadow. Even the first-years openly began to wander back into school after he threw them out into the playground, knowing that Cartwright would do nothing. He threatened all sorts of punishments, sometimes quite stupid ones – 'Right! You've done it now! One hour's detention every night until the end of term!' – but he never saw them through. Kerry stood in the playground and looked at Cartwright, who was watching the steady stream of fourth and fifth-years disappear behind the sheds. His face was a blotchy purple, and his bottom lip was sort of twisted. But when he toured the playground he gave the cycle sheds a wide berth. Kerry followed his example, not wishing to give Wayne any further opportunity to upset her.

It looked as if Billy was away from school yet again. What was she going to do, if she couldn't find him before Wayne got to her? She tried to imagine herself fighting Wayne. It just made her knees turn to water. Wayne liked to fight, and he knew how to hurt. Kerry had never fought anyone in her life. But she couldn't run away, either. Once, she had been a very fast runner, but Wayne could catch her easily with her leg the way it was now. Billy was a small hope; it might be that he was fed up with protecting her and would rather let the truth about his dad get out than fight Wayne. All the same, he was Kerry's only hope.

By dinnertime Kerry was feeling awful. Adrenaline seemed to be pumping around her body, making her feel restless and agitated. She wanted to run, to scream, to hit someone, anything to get rid of this awful feeling of fear and helplessness. Kerry and June were in different classes for technology, and when Kerry went to the cloakroom, where they usually met before going into dinner together, Kerry discovered that June was not there; she had gone into dinner already, a girl said, with someone else. Kerry did not feel like eating, and anyway did not want to go into the crowded dining room alone. Without really thinking about what she was doing, she picked up her kitbag and headed for the gym.

Sure enough, the place was deserted. The mats were down, the apparatus was fixed. Kerry stood for a long time at the door, looking at the equipment and seeing herself as she had been in the old days, vaulting up to the uneven bars and beginning her routine. She knew her best one by heart still, and even felt the tension in her muscles as she went through it in her memory: lifting, swinging, turning, back to the bar, stretching up, up; pausing, gaining control, perfectly still; then swinging, leaving the bar behind, twisting in the air before making contact again. Her hands, dusted with resin, felt sure and cool, the bar yielding slightly at her command. Kerry remembered it all, and longed for it so badly that she wanted to call out, to demand a putting-back of clocks so that she could have her chance again. The gym stayed silent.

Slowly, Kerry pulled her leotard out of her kitbag, letting the rest fall to the floor. She sat on a bench at the side of the gym, shielded from the door by the large vaulting apparatus, and took off her heavy shoes, and her socks. Swiftly, she changed into the leotard. Her breathing was quick and fast; she struggled to control it, as her trainer had shown her. She stood still, taking long, deep breaths. Then she tried a handstand.

It was not exactly successful. Her knee would not bend far enough, which affected her balance and made her roll over before she was properly straight. But when she tried again, allowing for the loss of movement by jumping slightly on to her hands at the start, it was better. She managed to get both legs reasonably together, and then went into a forward roll with legs straight. It hurt a bit, but not as much as she had feared. Next, Kerry tried flipping backwards. Again, the knee was stiff, but she found a way of moving which allowed for that. No doubt it looked very peculiar, but it gave Kerry such a sense of achievement that she went over to the parallel bars with growing confidence. Springing from her good leg, she gripped the bars and brought her legs up in front of her. The muscles tightened painfully, but she held on, getting the balance and the stillness. Her body was completely still. She felt a surge of triumph.

Kerry held the position one moment more and then let go, dropping to the mat as lightly as she could. She lay, flat on her back on the mat underneath the bars, eyes closed against the protesting muscles in her legs and abdomen, a smile on her face. She could do it. Now she knew. She could do it – not brilliantly, but well enough for a beginner. She would get better and better. For the first time since the accident, Kerry began to see herself not as a hopeless cripple but as someone who was suffering a temporary impairment. It was as if she had been struggling up a very steep hill with a heavy weight tied like a belt around her. Now she had reached the top, and the weight was gone. It was the best feeling she had ever known.

'Well, well, what have we here?'

The familiar, sneering voice mowed into her happiness and Kerry opened her eyes. Wayne stood over her. Kerry went to get up, but he placed his boot firmly on her chest and forced her back on to the floor.

'You move when I say so.'

The old terror seized Kerry and paralysed her. She lay, flat on her back, staring up at Wayne's evil, glowing face. He was crouching over her now. 'You haven't got much of a body, have you? I don't know what Billy sees in you – you're just like a stick insect.' He stared at the scars on her leg. 'What a mess! I don't suppose Billy's seen all that yet, eh? No wonder you wear your skirts so long. You should wear overalls for PE – not even Fats would fancy you without your clothes on.' He laughed.

Kerry, still unable to move because of the fear which gripped all her muscles, felt tears begin to creep out of her eyes and roll down her cheeks. She knew Wayne would really enjoy watching her cry, but she couldn't stop herself. 'Go away,' she said weakly. 'Mrs Tyson's only in the office – if you don't go away, I'll call out.'

'Bad luck,' said Wayne. 'I saw old Tyson going into the staff room on my way down, carrying a plate with sandwiches on it. Looks like you've been forgotten. Poor little spas.'

'Please, just go away and leave me alone,' whimpered Kerry.

'Yeah, all right. Soon as I've seen you doing your gym routine.'

'What?' Kerry was aghast.

'Yeah. This I've got to see – a cripple doing gym. I could do with something to brighten my day. You can get up now. What you gonna do first – the bars or the floor exercises?' He laughed again.

Kerry stayed where she was. 'No. I'm not going to do it,' she said savagely. Her body was starting to feel like hers again. 'Now push off, or I'll . . . '

'You'll what?' Wayne smiled when she didn't reply. 'Tell you what, Hollis – I'll help you up. Real gentleman, I am.' He suddenly grabbed her hair, making her scream as he hauled her to her feet. He put his other arm around her neck and clamped his hand over her mouth. Kerry bit it, and he pulled his hand away. Kerry lunged for the door, but Wayne still had her hair and he yanked her roughly back. 'You vicious little cow,' he said, and slapped her face so hard she could feel a little trickle of blood start in her nose.

Kerry's head felt as though she had been hit with a sledge hammer. Wayne let go of her hair, but caught both her arms before she could move away. His nails were biting through the leotard. 'Now,' said Wayne softly, 'I wanna see the cripple dance.' He let go of her, and stood with his arms folded and a poisonous half-smile. 'Go on, then.'

Kerry did not move. She flinched as he moved towards her. 'You can do what you like. I don't care any more. But I'm not doing anything for you. And when Billy finds out what you've done to me . . . '

'Billy? He's not exactly in a position to help you now, is he?'

'What do you mean?' said Kerry. 'As soon as he gets back to school . . . '

'Gets back?' Wayne's eyes narrowed. 'He hasn't

told you, has he? Whatever you've got going between you can't be much, if he didn't even tell you.'

'Tell me what?' said Kerry. Her heart was thumping so loud she could barely hear herself think.

'He ain't comin' back,' said Wayne.

'Of course he is,' said Kerry weakly.

Wayne smiled and shook his head. 'Ah, poor little kid. Got fed up with you, did he? Dropped you without even tellin' you? Naughty Billy. But he ain't comin' back to this school, so if you're looking for protection you'd better look elsewhere. Tell you what,' he finished, 'as a favour to Billy, for old time's sake, I'll look after you myself. I will give you my very special attention. How's that?' He moved forward and grabbed Kerry's hair again, twisting it in his hand and pulling her face close. 'Very, very special attention. Even cripples can be a bit of a laugh when they do what they're told. Which brings us back to this dance you were gonna do for me.'

Just then the gym door opened. Wayne immediately released his hold on Kerry's hair and adopted an innocent, interested expression, as though he had been listening to something Kerry was saying.

'What do you think you're doing, you two?' Mrs Tyson's voice was like ice. Behind her, a little gaggle of first- and second-years, in gym club leotards, stared at Wayne and Kerry.

'I was just talking to Kerry, Miss,' said Wayne smoothly. 'I didn't know where we was gonna meet after school.'

Mrs Tyson gave them both a long, suspicious look. 'What have you done to your face, Kerry? There's blood on your nose.'

'She whacked it on that horse,' said Wayne. 'One of the jumps went wrong, didn't it, Kerry? Good job I was 'ere to catch her, Miss, or she might have really hurt herself.'

'Kerry, is this true?' asked Mrs Tyson.

Kerry nodded, and stared down at the floor.

'If I'd known you were going to abuse my trust this way and set up the gym as a meeting place to fool around with your . . . friends, I would never have given permission for you to be here, Kerry. I'm very disappointed in you. Now get out, both of you. And you, Shaw, know very well that you're not allowed in here with outdoor shoes on. Go and report to the caretaker for litter duty.'

'Yes, Miss. See you after school, Kerry,' he said, for all the world as if they were the best of friends.

'Kerry? Are you all right?' The same old question.

'Yes, Miss. I'm fine. I'm sorry about Wayne.'

'Mmm. Kerry, are you sure there's not something you want to say?' Mrs Tyson looked over her shoulder at the little group of girls who were now starting to warm up. 'We can go into the office—'

'No. I'm just sorry, that's all. I'll go and get changed now.' Kerry picked up her things and went off in the direction of the changing rooms. She heard Mrs Tyson's brisk voice behind her. 'Into line, girls. Ready for the first exercise, one and two and. . . .' Taped piano music followed Kerry into the corridor, and was silenced again as the heavy swing door

89

closed behind her. Kerry limped into the changing rooms to wash her face, and examined herself in the large wall mirror. The red eyes were still full of tears, and a welt was forming across her face. Her nose had stopped bleeding before it reached full flow, and there was a smear of dried blood over her lip.

Worse than all this, though, was the feeling that the girl looking back at her as she wiped her face was not Kerry Hollis at all, but someone completely different. Kerry Hollis would never have allowed anyone to treat her this way. Kerry Hollis would have given as good as she got; creeps like Wayne Shaw and Billy Taggart would never have dared to touch her. This pale, trembling creature who was looking at her now had been born in the wreckage of a little red car at the side of a main road. Kerry Hollis had set out for the seaside, and this creature had taken her place during the journey.

Kerry felt a surge of hate so sudden and so powerful that it almost knocked her off balance. She hated God, or Fate, or whatever had made them choose that road at that time on that day. She hated her mother, who had been driving the car and must have done something stupid. Most of all, she hated herself for being crippled, and a coward. The pale face started to swim before her as more tears flowed. Kerry lifted her heavy shoe and struck the face in the mirror as hard as she could. It didn't go away. She hit it again. The face was red, and burning, but it still stared at her. Wildly, Kerry looked around the changing room. The rounders bats stood neatly in the rack. She grabbed one, and swung it at the mirror. There was a thud, the shattering of glass, and then the face was gone. There was only Kerry, sobbing alone in the deserted changing rooms in a shower of broken glass, clutching a bat.

9

It was a couple of seconds before Kerry came to
her senses and realized what she had done, and
then she was horrified. The mirror was completely
smashed up, and there was no way she would be
able to pass it off as an accident. She would be in
big trouble when Mrs Tyson saw it.

'Why did you do it?' they would ask her. 'Why?'
And what would she answer? 'I didn't like my face.'
Wonderful. She would be lucky not to be locked up;
perhaps she was going mad.

The only thing Kerry knew was that she couldn't
face up to telling Mrs Tyson, not at that moment.
She had to get away. Cautiously she opened the
door on to the corridor and peeped out. There was
no one in sight. She slipped out of the changing
rooms and walked towards the secretary's office.
The secretary went out to dinner, but the school
registers were kept in a cupboard just outside her
office. Quickly Kerry opened the door and searched
through until she found the register for Billy's form.
The names and addresses were listed in the front.

There it was: 'William Arthur Taggart, 49
Tanner Street'. A dark pencil line had been ruled

through it, and the words 'off roll' were scribbled in the margin. Kerry put the register back. It was true, then. Billy Taggart had left the school – but why? there had been no inkling of it the week before. Of course, there was no reason for him to have told Kerry about it. He had only been protecting her so she wouldn't tell about his dad, and if he was leaving he didn't have to worry about that any more.

Kerry thought about Wayne waiting for her at the park gates when school finished, and she thought about the smashed mirror which would be discovered any minute now. She tried to stand still and control her breathing, but the panic would not be stilled. The door to the side entrance, at the end of the corridor facing her, stood open. Outside, it was cold but bright and sunny, and freedom beckoned. Kerry stepped through the door and started off down the path. If she was caught she could just pretend she had volunteered for litter duty, but in fact no one stopped her. It was near to the end of the dinner hour now. Teachers were busy getting their books together, the prefect at the gate had gone in for a cup of coffee in the common room, and most of the pupils were in the playground on the other side of school. To Kerry, who had never before even contemplated playing truant, the whole thing was ridiculously easy.

Once outside, Kerry took off her blazer and stuffed it into her bag, along with the school tie. Now she was just an ordinary kid, dressed in a black skirt and a red jumper. Once she was on the other side of town, no one would know which school she came from. Kerry walked to the bus stop and jumped on the first bus which came along, although she had no idea where she was going.

'Well?' the conductor said. He was a bored-looking young man, not the type to ask awkward questions.

'Um – town centre, please,' said Kerry briskly. Thank goodness she still had her .dinner money. She had decided what to do, at least for a start. She would find Billy Taggart. Maybe by the time she did, she would have thought of a new way to make him help her against Wayne – threatening to let people at the new school know, or something like that. Kerry knew that Billy came from somewhere on the estate behind the little high street. Tanner Street must be there. She had never actually been into the estate, but she had passed it in the car. It was a large estate with long, straight roads criss-crossing each other; she would just have to start at the edge and work inwards until she found Tanner Street.

The Prospero Estate had been built just after the war, when there was a great boom in council-house building for the returning soldiers. Kerry imagined the houses had been quite attractive, once. They were all of red brick, two semis, then a terrace of four, then two semis again, all the way down each street. It was only when you got right into the estate that its shabbiness became overwhelming: row on row of peeling paint, neglected fences, gardens full of discarded wrappers and takeaway cartons from the nearby high-street shops. Even the pavements had large areas which were cracked and uneven, making Kerry stumble. Dogs seemed to roam where they wished, and owners either didn't read or chose to ignore signs about fouling the footway. Some of the houses had immaculate white net curtains and fresh paintwork, with fuchsia trees and tired roses struggling to bring cheer. But they seemed all the more sad for being swamped by a vast depression in brick. In general, Prospero Estate seemed to have given up hope.

The estate was built as a series of rectangles, each one facing on to a square of green. The first one that Kerry came across was larger than the rest, and a children's park occupied a corner of it. The swings had been wound round the top bar of the frame, making it impossible for children to use them, and the roundabout had several pieces missing. Two women were watching their children play on the slide and the climbing frame.

'Excuse me – do you know where Tanner Street is?' she asked.

'Across there,' one of them said, and pointed to the other side of the green.

'Thanks.' Kerry turned to cross the park. The sign of the street facing her when she reached the other side said 'Alma Street'. This started off another rectangle, facing on to a much smaller green area which had a skip parked firmly in the middle of it. An armchair, ripped and oozing foam, was poised on top of the refuse which threatened to spill over. An old woman sat in the window of one of the houses; she smiled and waved at Kerry as she went past. At the end of Alma Street was a T-junction. To the left, Caxton Street continued the rectangle round the green, and to the right Chapel

Street started off another rectangle. There was a small corrugated iron hut halfway down Chapel Street, announcing itself to be the Evangelical Centre. A big paper banner, spoiled by rain, fluttered above the doorway. 'Come to Me, Ye . . . ' – the next words were illegible. The little green square here was better cared for than the last, although the grass needed cutting. And there, at the end of Chapel Street and forming the bottom of the rectangle, was Tanner Street.

It occurred to Kerry for the first time that Billy and his mother might not even be in the house any more, or worse, that Billy's mother might be there on her own, and Kerry had no story as to why she was calling round, when she should be at school, to see a boy she thoroughly disliked. She paused at the end of Chapel Street to think. A curtain twitched; Kerry was watched suspiciously by a thin-faced woman in the house opposite. She moved on slowly, still trying to think.

Number 49 was scruffy, even by Prospero Estate standards. There was no fence and, although someone had made an effort to tame the lawn, the two little flowerbeds were overgrown with weeds and the path to the front door looked virtually unexplored. The paintwork was all a dull beige colour, and one of the windows upstairs was cracked right across. The afternoon sun tried in vain to penetrate the glass, which was dull with grime. It looked empty. Kerry pushed her way past the overhanging shrubs up to the front of the house. What should she do now?

The question was answered for her by Billy, who opened the front door and gaped at her.

'You! What the hell are you doing here?'

Someone in the house must have said something, because Billy turned and said over his shoulder, 'No, it's just someone from school.' He glowered at Kerry. 'What do you want?'

'I just want to ask you something.'

Billy was listening over his shoulder again, and took no notice of what she said. When he looked back at her his face was dark with fury. He advanced towards her, pulling the front door behind him. 'My mum wants you to come in,' he said. 'Just make sure you keep your trap shut. She's ill. If you upset her, I'll kill you with my bare hands, I swear to God I will.'

'Wh-what are you on about?' stuttered Kerry. She could see he meant what he said.

'You're a friend from school. You found one of my books and thought I might need it, so you've brought it round. Stick to that, amd make it quick. Or else.'

Kerry followed him through the narrow hall and into the living room. The heat in the room was almost stifling: a gas fire with all burners blazing stood in the fireplace. The room was cramped and stuffy, and not very clean. In a big armchair sat a thin old lady, in a bright pink dressing gown which made her sunken cheeks look even more withered. Despite the heat in the room – Billy was wearing jeans and a summer T-shirt – the woman had a blanket over her knees. She smiled at Kerry. It was a sweet smile, not at all the kind of smile Kerry would expect from anyone connected with the Taggart family.

'Hello,' said the woman. She beckoned Kerry to the footstool beside her chair, and Kerry sat down. 'Excuse me not getting up,' the woman said. 'I'm a bit poorly at the moment. Are you one of my son's friends?'

Kerry looked into the woman's face with a sense of shock. She had assumed it was Billy's grandmother, if she was any relative at all. Billy's mother could not possibly be as old as all that. The woman leaned back in the armchair. Her breathing was shallow, and now and then there was a curious soft rattling sound in it. Her skin was stretched like a piece of parchment over her bones, giving her the appearance of a newly covered skeleton. Her eyes, when she opened them again, were two dark, burning pools in the paleness of her face. Anyone could see that she was very ill, and that talking was an effort.

'What's your name?' asked Billy's mother. When Kerry told her, she smiled. 'The girl with the chocolate cake,' she said. 'Billy told me he went to tea with you . . . .' She ran out of energy, and closed her eyes again.

Kerry looked at Billy, who shook his head fiercely. He was standing in the doorway, leaning against the frame, watching the pair closely. Kerry knew that he was watching to make sure she did not say anything out of line. But Kerry would not do that to this poor, gentle woman, who didn't deserve to have a son like Billy.

'Billy, go and make the child a cup of tea. We must return the hospitality.'

Billy's face was like thunder.

'Oh, thank you, Mrs Taggart, but I can't stay, really. Another time, perhaps,' said Kerry politely.

'Another time – perhaps,' echoed Mrs Taggart, and there was something in her voice Kerry didn't understand.

Kerry touched the thin hand which reached out to pat her shoulder. 'I must be going,' she said awkwardly.

Mrs Taggart smiled. 'Yes. Billy will see you to the bus stop, won't you, Billy? He could do with a bit of time to himself.'

'Mum!' Billy's voice was almost a squeak.

'Go on – I want to sleep. Nothing will happen, Billy. Go on.' The dark eyes turned on Kerry for a moment. 'You're a good friend, are you, Kerry?'

'I hope so,' said Kerry. It seemed important to Billy's mother, and she could not bring herself to do anything other than lie to her.

'Take him out,' said the woman again, and closed her eyes. The gentle rattle became a regular, rhythmic beat. She was asleep.

Kerry stood up and faced Billy. She could feel his rage, almost as though it had real claws which could reach out and touch her. She had invaded his home, his private place, and he hated her for it. And yet he had told his mother about her, as if she were a friend. Why?

Kerry returned Billy's cold stare. He looked away first. Neither of them knew what to say. There was a long silence, then Kerry said, 'Come on, then.'

Billy shook his head. 'I can't leave her.'

'She wants you to.' Kerry felt an obligation to do as Mrs Taggart had asked. 'Look, will you just come into the garden? I really do want to ask you something.'

Billy nodded, and led the way through the kitchen into the back garden. This was a surprise. It was immaculately kept. A small, close-cropped lawn was bordered by flowerbeds. Trees and shrubs enclosed the garden, making it a private island of colour and birdsong. At the bottom of the garden, facing towards the house, was a white painted garden seat, surrounded by tubs of varying sizes with more flowers.

'It's beautiful,' breathed Kerry. 'Who takes care of it?'

'Me,' said Billy briefly. He met Kerry's look defensively. 'She sits at the window a lot – she loves the garden.'

They sat down together on the seat. Kerry was trying to sort out everything that was happening. She was sitting next to a thug, a bully who had made her life miserable. Yet he had made a garden for his mother. She looked at his coarse, broken-nailed hands as they fidgeted on his knees, and pictured them handling seedlings, watering living plants, nurturing, feeding, and coaxing small fragile things to grow tall and strong. None of it made sense.

'Your mother's very ill, isn't she?' Kerry said finally.

'Yes.'

'Is she going to die, Billy?'

'Probably.' Billy bowed his head. 'She's booked into a sort of nursing home next week. I don't think she'll come out again.'

'What about you?'

Billy's face hardened. 'Not that it's any business of yours, but I expect I'll go and live with my brother. He's in barracks, but the Army will help him find somewhere. They'll let me live on my own soon, but not yet. It's me brother or a home, the social worker says.' He turned on Kerry so quickly that she flinched. 'I expect you feel really satisfied, eh? Billy Taggart is getting his at last. Well, think on this, Hollis. I ain't coming back to school, that's for certain. You'll have to find another sucker to be your slave.'

The bitterness in his voice cut into Kerry like a knife. 'Why do you hate me so much, Billy?' she asked. 'I never did anything to you, did I? I'm the one who should hate you. What did I do to make you hate me?'

Billy gave a short, hard snort of laughter. 'I hate all your sort.'

'What sort?' When he didn't answer, Kerry touched his arm. 'What do you mean?'

Billy shrugged her hand away and stood up. He scuffed the ground with his boot. 'You think you're so great, don't you?' he said. 'You've got a mum and a dad who think the sun shines out of your arse, pots of money, nice house, smart car, holidays in the sun. You're a spoiled brat who expects everyone to like you, and feel sorry for you because of your leg. Well, you know what?' He turned and crouched by the seat, his eyes burning fiercely as

101

he put his face close to hers. 'I'd gladly have my whole bloody leg chopped off to get half what you have. I've never had a dad, not one who counted. My old man couldn't give a toss about any of us, and my mum had to do everything. She's never had a holiday in her life, nor even a new dress that hadn't already been worn by some snooty do-gooder. When they found out she had cancer, she was in hospital for ages. No one visited her, except me. They told my old man, and he didn't even apply for a special visit or send a card. She expected him to come, every day. She's given up now, though. She just sits there, being brave, not asking for anything.'

'But it wasn't anything to do with me,' said Kerry. 'I didn't even know. I didn't make it happen.'

Billy glared at her. 'I don't know why it happened, do I? Except you had everything and we had nothing. You mooned around all miserable and lost-looking, getting people to feel sorry for you, touchy with everyone about that leg as though it was the only thing that mattered. . . . I don't know why we done it. You just got on my nerves.'

'And that's it? I got on your nerves?' Kerry was shaking with new rage. 'I got on your nerves, so you lay in wait for me, night after night, using your fists on me to make yourself feel better? What kind of a reason is that?'

Billy shrugged. 'I told you, I don't know. Now shove off!' His voice was flat.

Kerry thought of the woman sitting in the house, waiting for the end of a life which had held little joy. Billy would be going to live with a brother he hardly knew, who might not even want him. The unfairness of it rolled together into a big lump in her throat. It was not fair that Billy's gentle mum was dying while his thuggish father lived; not fair that Billy had chosen Kerry to take it all out on; not fair that it was Kerry's mum who had crashed the car, but Kerry who had ended up with a twisted leg. She felt warm tears on her cheek.

'Don't start bleedin' crying,' said Billy. 'I don't need you feeling sorry for me, thanks all the same. Go home.'

But Kerry could not stop crying. 'To Wayne, you mean? Back to the bullying, night after night, knowing there's nothing I can do about it? That the only reason I get bullied is because I irritate someone?'

'Wayne would leave you alone if you just fought back, just once. But you stand there with that frozen snobby face, nose stuck up in the air – just stand up to him once.'

'So he'll go after some other poor kid instead? That's not what I want.'

Billy shrugged. 'I don't know what else to say.'

'Billy, why didn't you want Wayne to know about your dad? Would he really have cared about it?' said Kerry, changing the subject.

Billy shook his head. 'I doubt it. But Mum made me promise not to tell anyone. It was important to her. She was so ashamed of what he had done, it near killed her. She couldn't look anyone in the face. That's why we moved. She said we could start off afresh, as long as no one ever knew. When she got so sick, she kept bringing it up, making me promise over and over not to mention it. She wanted to make sure that the neighbours and that didn't know. Stupid, really; she's not used to tellin' lies, my mum. She told the school he was up in Scotland, workin' on the rigs. But when we moved in here, she told the neighbours he was dead. I couldn't say anything to Wayne, because of my mum. That's the only reason what you did worked.' He looked anxiously towards the house. 'Now you know all there is to know – so clear off, eh?'

They stood up together. Kerry wanted to wish him luck at his brother's place – suddenly she found she could not hate him any more. Perhaps she even felt a bit sorry for him. But there had been too much hurt just to sweep away. And a part of her, what she hoped was only a small part that she would never admit to June, was actually glad that Billy Taggart was suffering, and would suffer, more than Kerry ever had.

Kerry left him standing among the flowers in the garden, knowing that she would never see him again. She left with a mixture of feelings: the satisfaction of seeing him suffer; guilt, because of the satisfaction; sadness for the gentle woman who would soon be gone; fear of what would happen when she next saw Wayne; and a determination that, whatever happened, she was never going to be some stupid lout's victim again.

10

Kerry spent the next hour or so wandering around the shops, so that she would arrive home at the usual time. She did not know what would happen in afternoon registration. The usual thing was to ask someone to answer when your name was called, and hope the teacher didn't look up to check. But Kerry had not known she would be fleeing the school, and so had not arranged anything. Perhaps she could say she had been feeling sick, or that she had had pains in her leg and stopped to rest it. That would work, if Miss Jones had not hung around in the form room at the end of school. Kerry decided to go and see June, and ask her advice.

In fact, June was sitting in the park, waiting for her. She sprang to her feet as Kerry approached, looking very relieved. 'Thank goodness you're all right!' she gasped. 'I hoped you'd come this way. I've been out of my skull worrying. Where have you been? Miss Jones did her pieces.'

'Oh no,' groaned Kerry.

'Oh yes. When she called the register, I answered for you, but the old bag looked up just at the wrong moment. Then I said you had gone to the loo.'

'Thanks,' said Kerry.

'But it didn't work. She decided to wait – and when you didn't show, she kept me behind and gave me the full Jones treatment: responsibility to the school and to each other, the folly of telling lies, blah, blah.'

'Oh hell. What's she going to do?'

'She said she would telephone your mum and dad tonight to make sure you were all right, and see you herself tomorrow. She said to tell you not to get sick before then. In other words, be there or else.'

'They'll kill me,' said Kerry.

'No they won't – not unless they bore you to death. Your parents aren't the smacking sort. They'll sit you down, shower you with understanding and forgiveness, and give you a very long lecture on mutual trust,' grinned June. 'Give me a sore behind, any day.'

'How come you know them better than I do?' asked Kerry scathingly.

'Simple. You're a sweet-natured, good child who doesn't give anyone any trouble. I'll bet you've never done anything really bad. Now me, I'm in trouble so often I automatically size people up that way, so I know who I'm dealing with.'

'Maybe I can pull the phone out of the socket,' said Kerry.

'She'll only write – or call round. She's not daft. Anyway, it's no big deal. You skived off school, and not even for a whole day. They'll chew your ear and tell you not to be a naughty girl again. Be suitably penitent and that will be it, take my word for it.'

Kerry wished it were that simple. The mirror must have been discovered soon after she left, and they would be trying to find out who did it. Of course, there was no reason for anyone to suspect her, not right away. Anyone could have gone into the changing rooms, and no one saw her go in there. She knew it was her own guilty conscience that had made her think they would be hunting for her.

'Where did you go, anyway?' asked June curiously. 'I searched everywhere for you after lunch.'

'I went to see Billy,' said Kerry. She told June about Wayne in the gym at dinnertime – not the full details, and not about the mirror, because she was ashamed, but she admitted to being frightened enough to leave the school and go and find Billy. She told June about his mother, and Billy's care for her.

'Poor Billy,' said June. 'I can't say I ever liked him, and it's true he was a bully, but no one deserves that to happen.'

Kerry nodded. 'It was strange, you know,' she said. 'When I was in the garden with him, it was like part of me forgot who he was, or maybe he was so different . . . anyway, we squared a few things between us. He told me to stand up to Wayne. I know you told me that, too, but I didn't think I could do it. Then, seeing Billy and his mum made me think about life, you know, and how easy it is to lose it all. On the bus on the way back, I finally decided that Wayne Shaw is never going to hurt me again.'

'You're going to tell on him, then?' said June.

Kerry shook her head. 'That's what I should have done at the start, I can see that now. But I let it go too far. The only way to deal with Wayne is on his own terms. I'm going to get him.'

'You mean, a fight? He'll smash you to a pulp.'

'He might. But it won't be worse than what he's done to me so far, and I'll have the advantage of surprise. I'm scared of him, I have to admit that. But I'm angry, too, and I'm going to concentrate on the anger and try not to think about being scared. It's almost what they used to teach us in the gym team, you know, before a major competition. Concentrate on one thing, and everything else fades away.'

'I think you should tell,' said June, 'and let the teachers sort it out. It'll be just what they need to deal with Wayne once and for all. He's already been suspended, you know – this afternoon.'

'What for?' asked Kerry. 'For what happened in the gym?'

'Sort of – but not for what you think. Do you know what he did? He went into the girls' changing rooms and smashed up the big mirror with a rounders bat!'

'He didn't,' breathed Kerry. Her heart started to race.

'He did,' grinned June.

'How did they know it was Wayne?'

'One of the teachers saw him skulking about there after Mrs Tyson had thrown him out of the gym. He was mad because she put him on litter duty, so he smashed the mirror. He denies it, of course, but then he's Wayne Shaw, isn't he? You'd hardly expect a confession.'

Kerry was silent. Here was her golden opportunity. Not only would Wayne be punished for the mirror, he would be dealt with all the more harshly for what the Head would call barefaced lying. And he would experience all the rage of knowing he was innocent and having no one believe him. It would be a bit like the feelings of rage and frustration that he and Billy had made her suffer, so many times. Kerry could not help smiling at the prospect. Wayne would stew in his own juice.

'Whoops,' said June. 'Looks like La Jones has got there ahead of you.' She indicated Kerry's garden gate.

Kerry's mum was standing at the gate, and as they came nearer it was clear from the look on her face that Miss Jones had telephoned, as warned. 'Good luck,' said June. 'I think I'll go round by the road, if you don't mind.' She ran off back to the path leading to the park gates, as Kerry walked slowly over to her mother.

'Afternoon, Kerry,' said her mother evenly.

'Hello, Mum.'

'Good day at school?'

Kerry hung her head. 'I wasn't at school – not all day, anyway.'

'Indeed. Well, at least you have the courage to be honest about it. Actually, I know already. Miss Jones telephoned me.'

'Oh,' said Kerry.

'*Oh*. That's all you've got to say, is it, Kerry? *Oh*.' Her voice hardened. 'I've been worried sick since she called, wondering what can have happened. She says there was an incident in the gym at dinnertime – does it have anything to do with you skipping school?'

'In a way, I suppose.'

Mrs Hollis sighed. 'Let's go inside,' she said. 'I'll make some tea, and then I want a blow-by-blow account of where you've been this afternoon, young lady. And I want the truth.'

Kerry sat in the living room, trying to compose a story that would cause the minimum fuss. In the kitchen her mother was banging drawers and cupboards, and when she brought the tea in she was stony-faced. So much for June's idea of being washed in sympathy and understanding.

'Well?' asked her mother, as she handed Kerry a steaming cup of tea.

'Well, I just got fed up. Everything seemed to be getting on top of me, and I – well, I blew a fuse. I walked out.'

'Where did you go?'

'I went to Billy's house. Oh, Mum, it was awful.' Kerry told her mother the details of her visit to Billy and his mother.

Liz Hollis said nothing while Kerry talked, but she watched her daughter carefully. 'Is that it?' she asked finally. 'I have a feeling there's something else, Kerry. Why did you suddenly rush out of school without warning?'

Kerry thought about the mirror. The temptation to let Wayne take the blame almost overhelmed her. If they believed Wayne did it, they wouldn't be looking for anyone else. No one need ever know.

'*You* would know,' a voice inside her suddenly said. 'Every day, every time you passed Wayne or went into the changing rooms, you'd remember, and you'd look over your shoulder to see if anyone else suspected. Besides, all you're doing is sinking to the same level as him. You're just a coward, scared to own up.' Kerry sighed. She was fed up with being a coward; she had meant what she said to June.

With her luck, it would all come to light anyway, and she would be in even worse trouble for having kept quiet while they punished someone else. If it hadn't been Wayne, she would have confessed straight away.

She suddenly knew, as if someone had opened her up and poured in a golden stream of confidence, that she could deal with Wayne herself, as she should have done at the start. It was not Kerry Hollis who was the victim, but the pale girl who had stared out from the mirror. The only way to get rid of the pale girl was to reinstate Kerry Hollis, who would not be pushed around whether her leg was straight or crooked; a girl who had guts enough to own up when she had done something stupid.

Her mother listened to Kerry's confession as if she had been turned to stone. Kerry could see she was shocked, disbelieving, and she could not find words to tell her mother the very complicated thoughts that had led up to her aiming the bat at the mirror. She simply said that having to go slowly, and not being able to do gym properly, had finally got on top of her, and she didn't know why she'd done it, but she was sorry.

111

'Did you feel better afterwards?' asked her mother.

Kerry, who was expecting a big reaction, was taken by surprise at the question. She considered it. 'You know, I can't say I felt better,' she said, 'but I did feel calmer – as if the anger had gone through the bat and smashed to pieces with the mirror.'

'I see.' Her mother passed her hand over her forehead and brushed back her hair. 'Well, you'll just have to tell them that at school. You'll pay for the damage, of course. I wouldn't count on having much pocket money for a long time. You'll just have to tell them that you went crazy for a little while, and hope they understand. I'll take you in to school tomorrow – we both have an appointment with Miss Jones first thing.'

'I'm really sorry, Mum.'

Her mother nodded. 'Go upstairs and do your homework, Kerry.'

Kerry could hardly believe her ears. No rebuke, no long sympathetic speech – was that it? 'Don't you want to talk to me about it?' she asked.

Her mother smiled a horrid, bitter smile that did not reach her eyes. 'We should, shouldn't we? Maybe if we had more of a habit of talking things through in this family, you wouldn't have found yourself reduced to vandalism to express your feelings. Perhaps you could have told your father and me about them instead. Get along, now.'

Kerry looked back through the open doorway of the living room as she went up the stairs, and she saw her mother's bowed head as she wiped her eyes with a small white handkerchief. It was worse than any punishment Kerry could think of.

Upstairs, Kerry threw open her window and sank against the sill. She felt very mixed up. There was fear for tomorrow, sorrow for Billy's mother, anger at Wayne, and guilt and shame at having made her mother cry. Wayne, most of all, was to blame for all this unhappiness. Billy deserved to be punished for being a bully, but he was suffering for it now. Wayne, meanwhile, was getting off scot-free. It seemed no one could touch him. He could do what he liked, and never have to pay. The thought burned inside Kerry, eating away at her.

There were not many people in the park, although it was a dry day. The late afternoon sun was weak, and it was near to tea time. A mother who had been swinging her toddler strapped him back into his pushchair and walked towards the far exit; the couple who had helped Kerry before passed near to her house on their way out of the park by the other gates. Kerry watched without really concentrating.

Then her eye was caught by a movement over at the far gates: Wayne had just turned through them into the park. The gates were a long way off, and she couldn't see his face at all, but Kerry knew the swagger well enough. Wayne Shaw, striding into her park as though he owned it. Kerry fumed with rage. Kerry's mother was crying, and his best friend's mother was near to death, and yet Wayne Shaw moved with the ease of someone who hadn't a care in the world. The humiliation of that moment in the gym, when he had commanded her to dance,

113

returned to fill Kerry with redoubled rage. For Kerry knew that, had Mrs Tyson not come in that very moment, she would have obeyed Wayne. She would have danced for him, like a dumb creature, a thing in his possession. Did she have no pride left at all? 'Now,' said a voice. 'Now!'

Without stopping to think, Kerry crept down the stairs. Her mother was in the kitchen again, preparing dinner and waiting for Kerry's father to come home to the news of what their daughter had been up to. Quietly, Kerry slipped through the conservatory and out into the park. She moved as quickly as she could towards the gates on her side of the park, near which there were some thick bushes where she could hide; she would just have to hope that Wayne didn't look over in her direction and get suspicious.

Kerry stood behind a tree near the path, screened from it by shrubs and bushes. Her heart thumped against her ribs, and there was a strange ringing sound in her ears. She watched the curve in the path – he was sure to come this way. The park was a popular short cut to the youth centre from Wayne's estate, and that's probably where he was heading. She had no clear plan, except to spring out on him and hit him as hard as she could. Maybe she would be lucky, maybe not, but after today Wayne would at least know that Kerry Hollis was not going to lie down and die for him.

It seemed an eternity before she saw, through a veil of leaves, the familiar squat figure round the curve. She would wait for him to go past: she poised, ready. Wayne drew level with her, and then suddenly slowed his pace. He stopped just a couple of paces away, and pulled out a packet of cigarettes. Kerry saw that he was wearing Walkman headphones; he sang along as he searched his pockets for matches.

In the end it was all ridiculously easy. Wayne was so engrossed in what he was doing, and deafened by the personal stereo, that he had no idea someone was coming up behind him. The first he knew was a hard shove from behind which caught him unawares and sent him sprawling on to the black grit on the path. 'What the . . . ?' Kerry flung herself on him as he turned, without even noticing the surge of pain from her knee. She gathered his spiky hair in her two fists and thumped his head against the path. Wayne swore and grabbed at her, but she swiftly bashed his head again. His eyes glittered as he clutched her neck and her hair, trying to force her off, but Kerry clung on. She raised his head again and savagely beat it down to the ground, hearing the crunch of the gravel as it made contact. The grip around her neck loosened. She could not see Wayne's face now, only a bright red bar in front of her eyes. She could not hear anything either, except her own sobbing breath.

Someone was pulling at her now; whether it was Wayne or someone else, she could not tell. The strength started to seep from her arms, and the red bar across her eyes began to fade. She was aware of her father's voice. 'Kerry! For God's sake, stop it. Kerry!'

Her father had hold of her by the arms, and he dragged her away from Wayne. Wayne sat up, and

Kerry saw a red patch on his head, mixed with black gravel. His nose was bleeding, too, and he was screeching like a demented owl.

'You're a bleedin' head case, Hollis,' he screamed. 'You oughta be locked up.' He turned to her father. 'Just jumped out on me, she did. I didn't do nothin' – just jumped on me like a wild animal. She oughta be locked away for good.'

Kerry's father pushed Kerry away and stooped to examine Wayne's head. 'It doesn't look too bad,' he said. 'You may need a stitch, though. Come on, I'll take you to the health centre in the car.'

'Your kid could have murdered me!' screamed Wayne. He scrambled to his feet. Kerry moved towards him again, and he took a step backwards. 'Look at her! Keep her away; she's mad!'

Coolly, Kerry's father turned to look at his child. She was breathing hard. Bruises were starting to appear on her neck and her eyes were glazed with hatred. She did look a little mad. He turned back to Wayne.

'I don't know what's gone on here,' he said, 'but you can't ask me to believe she attacked you without reason.'

'She nearly bloody killed me!' said Wayne. 'What if you hadn't come along when you did?'

'You would probably be in the hospital,' said Kerry's father in the same tone of voice he might use to discuss the weather. 'You know, I thought there was something odd about the way you hung around the house, sending cryptic messages. I think you've been trying to frighten her. You picked the wrong girl to do that kind of thing to, young man.

My daughter knows how to take care of herself. You'd better stay well clear in future – now, do you want this lift to the health centre or not?'

Blood had begun to trickle into Wayne's mouth. He fingered his wound, and his eyes as he looked at Kerry were frightened, his face pale. Kerry looked at him with a sense of recognizing someone unexpectedly. Wayne's face looked like the face in the mirror.

'Kerry, go home. Go straight up to your bedroom, and stay there until I get back. You're going to rue the day you did this, my girl, whether you were provoked or not.'

'It'll be worth it,' said Kerry. She looked at Wayne, and moved towards him again, exulting to see him flinch slightly.

'Kerry, that's enough. Get inside!'

Kerry turned away from them and walked towards her mother, who stood a few metres off with her hands over her mouth. She looked back over her shoulder at Wayne, who was being helped to his feet by Kerry's father. They moved off together towards the gate. She must have kicked Wayne on the way down. He was limping badly.

Kerry was in big trouble, and she had a nasty feeling she was going to be paying for this day, one way and another, for a long time to come. But the sweetness of this moment would never be taken from her. She walked with a slight limp, but her head was high. Kerry Hollis was back.

Other great reads from **Red Fox**

Further Red Fox titles that you might enjoy reading are listed on the following pages. They are available in bookshops or they can be ordered directly from us.

If you would like to order books, please send this form and the money due to:

ARROW BOOKS, BOOKSERVICE BY POST, PO BOX 29, DOUGLAS, ISLE OF MAN, BRITISH ISLES. Please enclose a cheque or postal order made out to Arrow Books Ltd for the amount due and allow the following for postage and packing:
UK CUSTOMERS – please allow 30p per book to a maximum of £3.00
CUSTOMERS OUTSIDE UK – please allow 35p per book.

NAME _____

ADDRESS _____

_____

Please print clearly.

Whilst every effort is made to keep prices low, it is sometimes necessary to increase cover prices at short notice. If you are ordering books by post, to save delay it is advisable to phone to confirm the correct price. The number to ring is THE SALES DEPARTMENT 071 (if outside London) 973 9700.

Other great reads from **Red Fox**

Enter the gripping world of the REDWALL saga

REDWALL   Brian Jacques

It is the start of the summer of the Late Rose. Redwall Abbey, the peaceful home of a community of mice, slumbers in the warmth of a summer afternoon. The mice are preparing for a great jubilee feast.

But not for long. Cluny is coming! The evil one-eyed rat warlord is advancing with his battle-scarred mob. And Cluny wants Redwall . . .

ISBN 0 09 951200 9   £3.50

MOSSFLOWER   Brian Jacques

One late autumn evening, Bella of Brockhall snuggled deep in her armchair and told a story . . .

This is the dramatic tale behind the bestselling *Redwall*. It is the gripping account of how Redwall Abbey was founded through the bravery of the legendary mouse Martin and his epic quest for Salmandastron. Once again, the forces of good and evil are at war in a stunning novel that will captivate readers of all ages.

ISBN 0 09 955400 3   £3.50

MATTIMEO   Brian Jacques

Slagar the fox is intent on revenge . . .

On bringing death and destruction to the inhabitants of Redwall Abbey, in particular to the fearless warrior mouse Matthias. Gathering his evil band around him, Slagar plots to strike at the heart of the Abbey. His cunning and cowardly plan is to steal the Redwall children—and Mattimeo, Matthias' son, is to be the biggest prize of all.

ISBN 0 09 967540 4   £3.50

Other great reads from **Red Fox**

THE LONE WOLF ADVENTURES   Joe Dever

The Lone Wolf adventures are a unique fantasy gamebook series—each episode can be played separately or you can combine them all to create a fantastic role-playing epic. Hone your skills as a Kai Lord and learn your way around the treacherous peoples and lands surrounding your home of Magnamund as you progress from book to book.

The Lone Wolf series consists of 13 titles:

* Flight from the Dark
* The Caverns of Kalte
* Shadow on the Sand
* Castle Death
* The Cauldron of Fear
* The Prisoners of Time
* Fire on the Water
* The Chasm of Doom
* The Kingdoms of Terror
* The Jungle of Horror
* The Dungeons of Torgar
* The Masters of Darkness

The latest book in the series is:

LONE WOLF 13: THE PLAGUE-LORDS OF RUEL

In *The Plague-Lords of Ruel* you are the warrior Lone Wolf and your mission is to prevent the malevolent Cener Druids from releasing a deadly plague virus that will destroy all but their own kind. Of all the warriors of Magnamund only you can thwart their wicked plans—for only you possess the discipline of a Kai Grand Master.

ISBN 0 09 967690 7   £2.99

Watch out for new Lone Wolf titles coming soon!

Other great reads from **Red Fox**

The Maggie Series   Joan Lingard

MAGGIE 1: THE CLEARANCE

Sixteen-year-old Maggie McKinley's dreading the prospect of
a whole summer with her granny in a remote Scottish glen. But
the holiday begins to look more exciting when Maggie meets
the Frasers. She soon becomes best friends with James and
spends almost all her time with him. Which leads, indirectly,
to a terrible accident . . .

ISBN 0 09 947730 0   £1.99

MAGGIE 2: THE RESETTLING

Maggie McKinley's family has been forced to move to a high
rise flat and her mother is on the verge of a nervous breakdown.
As her family begins to rely more heavily on her, Maggie finds
less and less time for her schoolwork and her boyfriend James.
The pressures mount and Maggie slowly realizes that she alone
must control the direction of her life.

ISBN 0 09 949220 2   £1.99

MAGGIE 3: THE PILGRIMAGE

Maggie is now seventeen. Though a Glaswegian through and
through, she is very much looking forward to a cycling holiday
with her boyfriend James. But James begins to annoy Maggie
and tensions mount. Then they meet two Canadian boys and
Maggie finds she is strongly attracted to one of them.

ISBN 0 09 951190 8   £2.50

MAGGIE 4: THE REUNION

At eighteen, Maggie McKinley has been accepted for university
and is preparing to face the world. On her first trip abroad, she
flies to Canada to a summer au pair job and a reunion with Phil,
the Canadian student she met the previous summer. But as usual
in Maggie's life, events don't go quite as planned . . .

ISBN 0 09 951260 2   £2.50

Other great reads from **Red Fox**

**Haunting fiction for older readers from
Red Fox**

THE XANADU MANUSCRIPT
John Rowe Townsend

There is nothing unusual about visitors in Cambridge.

So what is it about three tall strangers which fills John with a mixture of curiosity and unease? Not only are they strikingly handsome but, for apparently educated people, they are oddly surprised and excited by normal, everyday events. And, as John pursues them, their mystery only seems to deepen.

Set against a background of an old university town, this powerfully compelling story is both utterly fantastic and oddly convincing.

'An author from whom much is expected and received.'
Economist

ISBN 0 09 9751801   £2.50

ONLOOKER   Roger Davenport

Peter has always enjoyed being in Culver Wood, and dismissed the tales of hauntings, witchcraft and superstitions associated with it. But when he starts having extraordinary visions that are somehow connected with the wood, and which become more real to him than his everyday life, he realizes that something is taking control of his mind in an inexplicable and frightening way.

Through his uneasy relationship with Isobel and her father, a Professor of Archaeology interested in excavating Culver Wood, Peter is led to the discovery of the wood's secret and his own terrifying part in it.

ISBN 0 09 9750708   £2.50

Other great reads from **Red Fox**

AMAZING ORIGAMI FOR CHILDREN
Steve and Megumi Biddle

Origami is an exciting and easy way to make toys, decorations and all kinds of useful things from folded paper.

Use leftover gift paper to make a party hat and a fancy box. Or create a colourful lorry, a pretty rose and a zoo full of origami animals. There are over 50 fun projects in Amazing Origami.

Following Steve and Megumi's step-by-step instructions and clear drawings, you'll amaze your friends and family with your magical paper creations.

ISBN 0 09 9661802   £4.99

MAGICAL STRING   Steve and Megumi Biddle

With only a loop of string you can make all kinds of shapes, puzzles and games. Steve and Megumi Biddle provide all the instructions and diagrams that are needed to create their amazing string magic in another of their inventive and absorbing books.

ISBN 0 09 964470 3   £2.50